The Prodigal Bride

BETH CORNELISON

MILLS
BOON®

First published in Great Britain 2011
by Mills & Boon, an imprint of Harlequin (UK) Limited,
Large Print edition 2011
Eton House, 18-24 Paradise Road,
Richmond, Surrey TW9 1SR

© Beth Cornelison 2011

ISBN: 978 0 263 21792 6

Printed and bound in Great Britain
by CPI Antony Rowe, Chippenham, Wiltshire

BETH CORNELISON

started writing stories as a child when she penned a tale about the adventures of her cat, Ajax. A Georgia native, she received her bachelor's degree in public relations from the University of Georgia. After working in public relations for a little more than a year, she moved with her husband to Louisiana, where she decided to pursue her love of writing fiction.

Since that first time, Beth has written many more stories of adventure and romantic suspense and has won numerous honours for her work, including a coveted Golden Heart award in romantic suspense from Romance Writers of America. She is active on the board of directors for the North Louisiana Storytellers and Authors of Romance (NOLA STARS) and loves reading, traveling, Peanuts' Snoopy and spending downtime with her family.

She writes from her home in Louisiana, where she lives with her husband, one son and two cats who think they are people. Beth loves to hear from her readers. You can write to her at PO Box 5418, Bossier City, LA 71171, USA or visit her website at www.bethcornelison.com

To Paul,
who has been my best friend and
my Valentine for twenty-five years.

Thanks to Rani Ogitani for lending
her name—again—to the babysitter
in this book, a character you first
met in TALL DARK DEFENDER.
Rani won the auction for this
opportunity through Brenda Novak's
Diabetes Auction, held each year in
May. Keep an eye out at this year's
auction for your chance to be a
character in an upcoming book!

Chapter 1

Pregnant.

Zoey Bancroft stared at the pink plus sign on the test stick, and her world tilted. She was going to have Derek's baby.

"Leapin' lizards," she muttered, her favorite expression since she'd starred as Annie in her junior high school's production of the musical. She sank onto the edge of the Las Vegas motel bathtub and pressed a shaky hand to her swirling stomach. *So maybe her nausea wasn't from a bad burrito after all.* Sucking in a slow deep breath, she tried to wrap her brain around the truth.

Pregnant. Judging by the date of her last period, she had to be two months along. *And how do you feel about this?* she imagined her sister Holly asking her.

Stunned. Confused. Scared.

And *alone.* Derek had made a hasty retreat when she'd suggested she might be carrying his child. *The jerk.* She'd believed in him, sacrificed for him, shared herself with him. But when she needed him most, he'd left her, unwilling to take responsibility for his child.

The whoosh of blood filled Zoey's ears. Again her world tipped, until it listed precariously over a black void. A flutter of panic beat its wings in her chest. She'd believed Derek was her future. She'd thought herself in love with him, an illusion that had begun cracking weeks ago. What she'd wanted to believe was love, she saw now, had just been a fantasy, just the latest wrong turn in her search for her place in the world. Derek had left her dangling over this fathomless pit of isolation and fear. How could she have been so blind?

Her father had been right about Derek. She'd argued with her father, severed ties with her family and defended Derek and her choice to travel the country with him as he competed in poker tournaments, hoping for his big break. Dejection and regret settled in her chest like a cold rock when she saw how wrong she'd been to trust Derek. He'd used her, strung her along, dumped her when her money ran out and the chips were down. Just as her father had predicted.

She frowned as she stared in the mirror on the back of the bathroom door. The green-eyed reflection gazing back at her sought answers she didn't have. Her appearance wasn't substantially different from normal. She didn't look like she thought a mother-to-be should. Instead of a healthy glow, her freckled cheeks seemed pale in the harsh fluorescent light. But wan complexion aside, the auburn-haired woman who stared back at her was the same lost-and-searching soul who'd been looking for herself, auditioning different life roles for all of her twenty-four years. She huffed her disgust.

Another screwup. How typical of you.

Okay, this baby wasn't planned, but it didn't have to be a problem. Shaking off the self-censure, Zoey took a deep breath. Babies were good. She liked babies. She could take care of a baby...even if she was alone. Wisps of apprehension tickled the back of her neck. *Could she do this alone?*

She conjured an image of the people she loved most, people she'd depended on in the past— her parents, her sisters...her best friend, Gage.

Maybe her horrible blindness and subsequent fight with her parents over Derek meant she was estranged from her family, but ever since they'd became friends in junior high, Gage had always been there for her. She didn't know what she was going to do with her life now, but she knew who had her back. She knew who she would call....

On the back porch of Gage Powell's Lagniappe, Louisiana, home, the cordless phone he'd set on the umbrella table trilled in the fading autumn sunshine. Gage propped his rake against the trunk of the large oak and jogged toward the porch.

"G-Gage?" the female caller rasped when he answered. The woman's voice was choked with tears. Tears usually meant the caller was his older sister. But the voice wasn't Elaine's.

"Yeah?"

"He left me. I told him about the baby, and he left me!"

Once she spoke again, Gage recognized the voice, even through the muffle of tears. Instantly he jerked to attention, his body humming and his heart thudding like it had the first day he'd met her in junior high school.

Zoey Bancroft. His best friend. First lover. Secret love.

Fiery auburn hair and a personality to match. His heart ached picturing tear tracks on her beautiful freckled cheeks, her green eyes red from crying.

With a glance to the yard to check on his niece, Pet, who was still playing on the swing set he'd finished assembling last weekend, Gage sank onto a patio chair. "Zee, what's going on? Who left? What baby?"

She sniffled loudly. "He told me he didn't want a baby, and if I kept it, he was outta there. Can you believe he'd say something so awful?"

A chill washed through Gage. "Back up, Zee. Are you saying you're *pregnant?*"

"Yes," she squeaked. "And alone. Derek left."

Derek. Gage curled his fingers into fists and gritted his teeth. He'd known the guy was no good, would end up hurting Zoey. But Gage had tried to be supportive, tried to keep his mouth shut when Zoey gushed in her random phone calls about the guy's poker tourneys and their life on the road.

Zoey's father had tried to warn her what kind of cretin Derek was, and the resulting argument had caused a rift in the Bancroft family that had lasted more than two years. Zoey had even missed her sister Paige's wedding earlier this summer. Paige's *almost* wedding. But then

Gage was just as glad Zoey hadn't been in the line of fire that day...

He shook his head to clear it and focused on what Zoey was saying.

"—went down to the bank to check, and it was true! My savings is empty. My entire inheritance from Grandpa Bancroft is gone! And the balance of our checking account is a negative because of an overdraft and fines. I actually owe the bank two hundred dollars!"

Acid puddled in Gage's gut as he sorted out what Zoey was telling him. "So...wait. You're pregnant. And you have no money. Zero. None. Derek cleaned you out, then abandoned you?"

"Yes." Another squeak. More sobs. "I told him the PIN for my ATM card—and yes, before you say it, in hindsight, I see that wasn't the smartest idea. But until recently, he gave me no reason not to trust him."

Rage, horror and grave concern swam together through Gage, leaving him shaking as he tried to absorb Zoey's circumstances. Her zest for life, her reach-for-the-stars passion and restless energy were part of what made her so special to him. She'd imbued him with the same hopefulness and never-say-die attitude many times in high school when his circumstances made him want to give up. She'd always been a fresh breeze in his stale life.

But she'd been burning her candle from both ends so long that he'd feared eventually it would catch up with her. Just as he'd known he'd be there to help her pick up the pieces, the way she'd always been there for him. Even though they'd never lost touch throughout her travels, whenever her life was in transition, she'd come back to Lagniappe, and they would reconnect, rebuild the bond that made them such good friends. And each time she flitted off on her next exploit, his heart cracked a little more.

He drew a breath, gathering his thoughts. "Okay, don't worry. We'll figure this out together."

"I hope you ate your Wheaties this morning, 'cause I'm fresh outta ideas."

His cheek twitched with a grin. At least her wry sense of humor was still in place. Her ability to make him smile in even the direst situation had helped him endure his own past crises and boded well for her resilience with her own troubles.

In his yard, Pet was kicking at the pile of leaves he'd just raked, scattering them to the four winds. He didn't care. She was having fun.

First things first. "Where are you? Are you somewhere safe?"

"I'm at our motel, but I don't know how long I can stay here before the manager kicks me out and demands payment for the room."

"What motel? Where?"

"In Vegas."

He heard a pounding in the background.

Zoey gasped. "Hang on. Someone's at the door." Gage heard the rustle of sheets, the creak of bedsprings. "It could be Derek. Maybe he came back to apologize—"

The hope in her voice slayed him. Her optimism was a double-edged sword. She'd kept him focused on the positive throughout high school, but it made her vulnerable to guys like Derek. Was she going to give the creep another chance? After he'd shown his stripes by leaving her, shirking his responsibility to his baby, stealing all her money? He wanted to shake Zoey. "Wait, Zee. Don't let him in. You deserve b—"

A loud crash and Zoey's startled scream cut him off.

Gage's pulse leaped, and he lurched from the patio chair. "Zoey, are you there?"

"Who are you? What do you want?" Her voice sounded distant as she talked to whoever was at the door. Gage recognized the tremble of fear in her tone.

The gruff rumble of a male voice answered her, too quiet for Gage to understand.

"That's Derek's problem, not mine."

Gage paced across his porch, agitation nipping him. "Zee, who is it? What's happening?"

Another mumble of a deep voices.

"I don't have it. No!" Her pitch rose, filling with panic. "Stop! Get out, or I'll call the cops!"

"Zoey!" Gage yelled.

She cried out, sending Gage's blood pressure into the stratosphere. "Zee, answer me!"

A crackling sound blasted his ear, followed by a deafening silence.

Then a dial tone.

He clutched the phone to his ear like a lifeline to her, anxiety climbing his throat. "Zoey!"

But she was gone.

He quickly punched in her cell phone number and waited while it rang...and clicked over to voice mail.

"Zoey here. You know what to do," her message chirped in the bright, carefree tone that characterized the woman he'd fallen in love with years ago. Spontaneous. Mischievous. Full of life.

"It's me, Zee. I'm worried about you. Call me." His voice quaked, but he didn't care. Zoey had seen him worse off. Much worse.

"Look at me, Uncle Gage!" Pet called from the yard.

He raised his head to find his niece hanging upside down from the swing set. His five-year-old niece was a lot like Zoey. Wild. Full of energy. Fearless.

"I'm a monkey!" the dark-haired imp giggled as she swung from the top bar.

"Be careful, Squirt. Don't fall." One personal emergency at a time, please.

He might be a firefighter, a first responder, handling crises in the community for a living, but in his private life, Gage could juggle only so much. Taking custody of his niece while his sister dried out and put her life back together already consumed most of his energy. Now Zoey was in trouble.

He had no use for a trip to the E.R. tonight with Pet. *Been there. Done that.*

Dividing his attention between the phone and his niece, Gage redialed Zoey's number.

Again the call kicked over to her voice mail. "Zoey here. You know what to do."

But he didn't know. As he had much of his life, Gage felt himself sinking into uncertainty, worried about the people he loved. What was he going to do with Pet? With his sister?

And how the hell was he supposed to help Zoey?

Chapter 2

Zoey gaped at the thug who'd crushed her cell phone under his boot heel when she'd threatened to call the police. The guy wasn't scary in the traditional sense—in fact she'd call him more goofy-looking than intimidating. He had a zigzag buzz cut and a pierced eyebrow that added to his trying-too-hard-to-look-tough appearance. No, what bothered Zoey were his arms, specifically the tracks of needle marks up and down his skin. If he was high, he could be dangerously unpredictable.

With a jerk on the cord, he disabled the motel room's landline, as well.

How could Derek have done business with these cretins? And how could she convince them that she had no more money than Derek did to pay off Derek's debts?

"You don't want to call the cops, 'cause that would piss me off. And I'm not someone you want pissed at you." He aimed a finger at her and narrowed his eyes to slits. "It's real simple. Either tell us where Derek is or give us the twenty grand he owes us."

Zoey choked. "Twenty grand? He told me it was just a couple thousand!"

The guy who'd stomped her cell phone jammed his face in hers. "Your boyfriend lied. And the price goes up every day he's late payin'. Interest, you know."

His breath smelled of cinnamon gum, and Zoey pulled a face. What should have been a refreshing scent turned her stomach coming from him. "Look, Derek and I split up. Your beef with him is not my problem. I don't have any money. He stole it all from me, so—"

A stinging smack landed on her cheek, and she gasped in shock and pain.

Mr. Cinnamon-Breath shook out the fingers in his hand. A hissing-snake tattoo on his forearm seemed to writhe as his muscles flexed. "I told you not to piss me off."

Zoey raised her chin defiantly. He was ticking her off, too. "I don't have—"

He grabbed her wrist and jerked her close. "Derek told us you came from money. You can get that twenty thou and a whole lot more from your family."

A chill slithered through her. Dread knotted her gut knowing this guy would likely extort any sum of cash he could from her through fear and intimidation. *Her family's money.* She couldn't let this guy's menace hurt her family. Squaring her shoulders, she dug deep for the courage to stand up to this bully. "My family disowned me two years ago when I hooked up with Derek. They won't give me a cent." She waved a hand toward the dingy motel room bed. "Do you think I'd be living like this if I had a cash flow from my parents?"

"You got credit cards, don't you?"

"I, uh—" Her gaze darted to her purse and back, her spirits rising. Her emergency credit card! After getting in a load of debt in high school, from which her parents had had to bail her out, Zoey had sworn off credit cards, cut them up. Except for one. The emergency Visa. Well, this was an emergency, right?

Except the thug's gaze moved to her purse, too. Uh-oh.

"Hey, Viper, a cop just pulled in up at the front office," his cohort said from the door. "Time to go."

Viper—his moniker no doubt the reason for his tat, or vice versa—stiffened and snapped his gaze toward the door with a grumbled curse. Returning his narrowed glare to Zoey, Viper backed toward the door. "You seem like a smart girl. Use those smarts to come up with my money. Meantime, we'll just take this." He grabbed her wallet—with the emergency credit card and what little cash she had—and stormed out without closing the door.

Hiccuping a half sob, Zoey slid to the floor.

She touched her throbbing cheek and shivered. Cheesy theatrics or not, Viper and his cronies scared her. She had no doubt they'd return, and they'd hurt her if she didn't come up with the money they wanted.

She could, of course, still go to the cops. But how much evidence could she give them? What could the cops really do? This was Las Vegas, for crying out loud. Loan sharks had to be as common and pesky as flies in this town. The cops might swat at one, but another would buzz around a few minutes later, until the police accepted them as part of the landscape.

Dragging herself to her feet, she staggered to the door and slammed it shut. After throwing the feeble security lock and latching the chain, she stumbled to the bed and curled into a ball. She wanted to call Gage back, tell him what had happened, but her phone was in pieces thanks to Viper's boot, the room phone disabled.

She tried to push aside the jitters Viper and his pals had stirred. She had to figure out what to do, how to get herself out of her circumstances. Without money, she couldn't even buy a bus ticket home. She was stranded in Vegas. Her phone was ruined. She had no job, no boyfriend. And she was pregnant.

Her dire straits pressed down on her, nearly suffocating her. When tears pricked her sinuses, she closed her eyes as, like Dorothy in Oz, she dreamed of home. Of Lagniappe. Her family.

As much as she wanted to call her parents or her sisters for help, her pride wouldn't let her. She'd been a disappointment to her overachieving family most of her life. The black-sheep sister. The daughter with the penchant for trouble. She couldn't bear the thought of telling them how royally she'd screwed up again, especially because her father had predicted Derek would lead her to ruin.

Her returning to Lagniappe penniless, unwed and pregnant would cause whispers in her parents' social circle that would haunt them for years. She'd hurt her family enough with her rebellion, her stubbornness, her rash decisions to last them a lifetime. No. Asking her family to bail her out again was not an option.

Her gaze drifted to the broken pieces of her

phone, and a deep, caring voice filtered through her memory. *Okay, don't worry. We'll figure this out together.*

Gage. Her heart squeezed as her best friend's face swam in her mind's eye. His crooked smile, his puppy-dog brown eyes and scarred chin, courtesy of his abusive father. Gage had been her best friend since eighth-grade drama class. She'd taken drama because it gave her a creative outlet. He had been in the class because of a scheduling mix-up. But his handiness with tools and woodcraft proved valuable in building sets, so he'd stayed in the class.

Zoey, ever the extrovert, had struck up a conversation with the quiet, gangly stagehand and been drawn to his quirky sense of humor. Later, as their friendship deepened and bonds of trust formed, she'd learned his humor was a shield that hid a home life she wouldn't wish on her enemies. The Bancroft home had become Gage's sanctuary, his escape when his home life was at its toughest, and Gage had become Zoey's safe harbor when she felt adrift, struggling to live up to the high-water mark her sisters set and always falling short. When her wanderlust after graduation had grown wearisome, she'd returned home and found Gage waiting for her, willing to forgive her rash disappearance from his life after one life-changing night that had shaken her to the core...

Gage shrugged his shoulder in an uncomfortable contortion to keep his cell phone against his ear, waiting for the bank representative to take him off hold, while he poured a bowl of raisin bran for Pet and doused it with milk.

Pet curled her lip in disdain. "What's that?"

"Supper. Eat."

"I don't like it."

"You haven't tried it." He shoved the milk back into the refrigerator and shifted his cell to a more comfortable position. Elevator music droned in his ear.

As soon as it was clear Zoey wasn't going to answer her cell, Gage had called the police department in Las Vegas, hoping to send the cavalry to her rescue. But not having an address to give them, there was nothing they could do.

Plan B meant finding Zoey himself. Whatever it took. And fast.

"It has raisins. I'm 'lergic to raisins."

"You're not allergic to raisins."

"Am so."

"Are not. Eat."

"I don't want this. I want chicken nuggets," Pet grumbled and poked out her lower lip.

Gage gritted his teeth and battled down his growing frustration. He refused to lose his temper with Pet. She wasn't the reason for his agitation or the acid gnawing his stomach. His worry over Zoey and his inability to get in touch with her was his chief aggravation at the moment.

"We're out of chicken nuggets, and I'm not making mac and cheese again. You need vitamins." He tapped the cereal box. "See here? This says it's fortified with vitamins. It's healthy."

"Ice cream's healthy. It has milk."

"You can't—"

"Sir?" the bank employee said as she came back on the line. "We're not allowed to disclose private financial information, even to family members. I'm sorry."

Shooting his niece a warning look, Gage aimed a finger at the bowl of raisin bran as he paced out of the kitchen. "But this is an emergency. I'm not looking for account numbers or balance information, I just need to know where Zoey Bancroft might have made ATM withdrawals or credit-card purchases in the past couple days. Are there any motel charges?"

"I'm sorry, sir. I can't give out that information."

Gage pinched the bridge of his nose. He was losing valuable time arguing bank policy with the woman. "All right, all right. Thanks anyway." *Thanks for nothing.*

He thumbed the disconnect key, and his shoulders sagged. He was getting nowhere, while somewhere in Las Vegas, Zoey was alone, pregnant, broke and quite possibly in danger.

He had to act. He couldn't sit here and wait for word from her that might never come. Already nearly an hour had passed since her call.

Riley Sinclair owed him a couple days from

the last time Gage had covered Riley's shifts at the fire station. If he could—

"Yuck!" Pet shouted from the kitchen. "Raisins are gross!"

Damn. Even if he could get the time off, what was he supposed to do with Pet?

Another firefighter at the station, Cal Walters, had referred him to a babysitter that he used on the days he worked. Because his schedule at the fire station meant he was gone overnight, his sitter, Rani Ogatini, was used to extended stays with Pet.

"Uncle Gage!"

He pulled his address book out of a stack of bills on his desk and flipped through it, looking for Rani's number. "We don't have anything else until we go to the store. Eat the cereal."

Pet gave a theatrical groan of discontent. *Drama queen.* Like someone else he knew.

Except this time. He'd heard real fear, real misery, real desperation in Zoey's voice when she'd called.

Zoey needed him. Now. Time to act.

Punching Rani's number into his cell, Gage set his plan in motion.

Zoey curled into a ball on the bed at the emergency shelter and tried to shut out the noise from the street. She'd cried so much in the past twenty-four hours that she'd wondered if her contacts might float away. Then she'd be blind as a bat on top of everything else. Her stomach growled, even though she'd had breakfast in the shelter's dining hall. The baby apparently needed to be fed every two hours or her hunger and nausea returned. She'd gone out earlier today looking for a job—anything she could do for a few weeks, until she could earn enough money to get back to Lagniappe—but found nothing. She'd called to have her Visa account canceled so that Viper couldn't run up charges on it, and because of her shaky credit history, a new account would take up to three business days to be approved. She was flat-broke until then.

Knowing Viper could come back to the motel room at any time and knowing she needed food and shelter, for her baby if nothing else, she'd swallowed her pride and headed to the address for an emergency-aid shelter she'd seen at a bus stop. Per the rules of the shelter, she could stay only two nights before finding another place to stay. But for at least one more day she had a place to regroup, a base from which she could look for work and a kitchen where she could get a hot meal. A charity shelter felt like a last resort, but because of her baby, she knew she needed nourishing meals and safe housing. She had that here. For now.

When she thought of going home, her tail between her legs, hoping her father would forgive her foolishness, a bubble of wounded pride swelled in her chest. Admitting she'd been wrong about Derek hurt. Letting her family see how low she'd sunk grated. But like the prodigal son of the Bible, if she didn't find a job soon, she'd have to dig up some humility and face the I-told-you-sos. For her baby.

The last thing she wanted was to hurt her family. She hated the idea that her recklessness would bring shame to the Bancroft name and give her parents more reason to be disappointed with her. If she had other options, she'd jump on them. But she was at a dead end.

Her pregnancy reared its head with seesawing nausea, and she wrapped her arm around her middle and groaned. "Please, little one, Mommy's got enough to deal with without you making me sick." How could she be hungry and nauseous at the same time? Yet she was.

A loud pounding on her room's door reverberated off the thin walls. Zoey sat up, holding her breath, her heart racing.

"Zoey?" a male voice called.

She froze. It sounded like—

Rolling off the bed and clambering to her feet, Zoey raced to the door and tore it open. Without hesitation, she launched herself at the man standing across the threshold.

"Gage!" Tears of joy flooded her eyes as she wrapped a tight hug around his shoulders—shoulders far broader than she remembered. In high school, he'd been downright spindly.

He stumbled back a step before catching his

balance. "Oh, thank God, Zee! Are you all right? You're not hurt or sick or—"

He squeezed her tighter, and she felt the shudder that raced through him. Wiggling free of his zealous embrace, she nodded and swiped at the moisture in her eyes. "I'm so glad to see you! I would have called you this morning, but they have some kind of block on the house phone so you can't call long distance, and that cretin Viper smashed my cell phone," she gushed without taking a breath. "I didn't have enough money for a meal, much less a bus ticket home, so I had no choice but to come here. I've been so alone. So scared. But now..." Excitement spiked in her again. "Now you're here and...ohmigod, I'm so glad to see you! But..." she paused and blinked her confusion, "...h-how did you find me *here?*"

Gage flashed his crooked grin and chuckled. "Take a breath, Zee. You're gonna pass out if you don't breathe between paragraphs."

She soft-punched his arm, then took a hard look at him. He had a couple of days' growth of dark brown beard. His mahogany eyes were rimmed with red. Lines of fatigue creased his face, and hair that hadn't seen scissors in too long curled in rumpled disarray. He'd never looked better to her. In fact, he looked...sexy. She shook off the unexpected reaction and opted for the safer, familiar ribbing that had served her so well in high school.

"Jeez, Gage, you look like crap."

He arched an eyebrow and grunted. "Gee, thanks." He took her elbow and guided her inside, closing the door and frowning when he saw the dingy room. "You've been living *here?*"

"Only for the last day. Since Derek pilfered all my money for his gambling debts, free is all I can afford." She crossed her arms over her chest and swallowed hard to loosen the knot of emotion in her throat. "I know what you're thinking. Oh, how the mighty Bancroft princess has fallen."

He stepped closer and brushed a tangled wisp of her hair behind her ear. "That's not what I was thinking. I was thinking it's a good thing I came after you. I was thinking how grateful I am that you're safe. That piece of conversation I overheard with the guy I can only assume was this Viper you mentioned scared the bejeezus out of me. For all I knew, you'd been beaten and were lying bleeding to death somewhere."

Almost of its own volition, her hand lifted to her eye where Viper's slap had left a small bruise. Mistake. Gage narrowed his gaze and pulled her closer to the bathroom light.

"Gage, it's nothing. Don't—"

He tensed, his mouth firming to a taut line. "Son of a—! He did hit you, didn't he?"

"Gage, chill. I'm okay."

Jamming a hand in his hair, he turned to stalk toward the bed where he dropped heavily onto the mattress. "It's not okay, and you know it. A man never has the right to hit a woman." His face paled, and his gaze shot back to hers. "Especially not a pregnant woman. Are you… Is it—"

She grinned at his obvious discomfort with her pregnancy. "If my morning sickness is any indication, the baby's fine. And for the record, morning sickness is a grossly erroneous term.

I'm sick all day. All. Day. Especially when I don't eat."

Gage dragged a hand down his stubbled cheeks, and the scratchy sound of his beard abrading his palms sent a tingle down her spine. Had his jaw always been that square? Zoey tilted her head and studied him. No, he definitely had a more masculine cut to his cheeks and chin now. And his exercise regimen with the fire department had helped his chest and shoulders fill out. Her breath caught in her lungs. *Sexy* filtered through her mind again before she could stem the absurd thought. This was *Gage,* for Pete's sake.

He lowered his brow in a scowl. "Stop looking at me like that. I know I look like crap. You told me that already. But I haven't slept in more than forty-three hours."

Zoey straightened. "What? Why not?"

He made a face that said the answer should have been obvious. "Like I was going to sleep before I found you. After driving through the night to get here, I spent the last twenty-two hours visiting every damn motel in Sin City with your picture, trying to track you down. When I explained the situation to one desk clerk, she suggested I try the shelters, too…which is what led me here."

A warm fuzzy feeling flooded her chest. "You mean you drove out here with no idea where I was and have been flashing my mug shot around all day to find me?"

He gave a casual shrug.

More tears pricked her eyes. Damn, but pregnancy made her emotional. "That is so Daniel Day Lewis from *Last of the Mohicans*. 'Stay alive, whatever may occur. I will find you!'"

He snorted. "Whatever."

Zoey laughed and rushed to his side, throwing her arms around him and pressing a kiss to his bristly cheek. "My hero!"

He scoff-laughed. "Give me a break."

"You know that is my favorite movie of all time. You can't tell me that scene didn't come to you during the whole drive out here or anytime during your motel search."

"No, Zee. It didn't." He faced her, his eyes a shade darker than normal. Under his piercing stare, her stomach performed a giddy flip-flop. "I was way too preoccupied with wondering if I would be too late to help you, deciding what to do once I found you, what to do if I didn't find you..."

She squeezed his hand between hers and gave him her brightest smile. "You are the dearest, sweetest guy ever. I'm so lucky you're my friend."

A muscle in his jaw twitched, and he shifted his gaze away. "Yeah, well..."

Shoving to her feet, Zoey tugged his arm and hauled him off the bed. "Speaking of which... if you want to help me, I'll tell you what you're going to do. You're going to take me to the nearest restaurant that has cheeseburgers and buy me lunch. I'm famished!"

Gage rubbed his eyes with the heels of his hands. "Yeah, okay. But then can I nap for a while? I think I could sleep for a week."

"Yes. You can sleep when we get back," she said with a laugh. "Whatever you want. I'm so glad to see you, I'd French-kiss Wayne Newton if you asked me to."

Gage staggered toward the door with a groan. "Please, don't. I'm really tired of seeing you hook up with guys who are all wrong for you."

Gage watched Zoey wolf down a cheeseburger and fries, and he listened patiently as she filled him in on the details of how Derek the Ass had used her and left her stranded.

"How am I supposed to face my family?" Her voice warbled as she dragged a French fry through mustard—that habit still turned his stomach—and sent him a look of misery. "My dad all but disowned me. My sisters have their perfect lives with men who actually love them, and my mom will want to fuss over me like I'm some errant child who can do nothing but mess things up," she scoffed. "And maybe that's who I am. The family screwup. The problem child. I can't blame them for being ashamed of me."

Gage sat straighter and scowled at her. "Your family is not ashamed of you, Zee. They love you, no matter what." *Just like I do.* He bit his tongue. He'd almost said the last aloud. And wouldn't that send her running for the hills, screaming?

"Maybe before. But this time…I really messed up. I'm knocked up and broke. Not a lot to be proud of there. My dad was right about Derek. So how do I go home with any dignity at all?"

"Well, maybe you don't." He jabbed at the ice in his glass with his straw, watching her expression carefully. "Maybe you go home with humility and a lesson learned."

"If I didn't have to put my baby's needs first, I'd stay here and work as a topless cocktail waitress in some dive rather than be a burden and humiliation to my family."

Gage knew her well enough to know she wasn't serious, but he still pictured her delivering drinks topless…and his libido kicked hard. Then he imagined the grubby drunks she'd be serving ogling her, and his blood pressure spiked.

She gave a humorless laugh. "Can't you just see that? Me, pregnant out to here—" she held her hand a foot from her belly "—and serving drinks topless?"

Gage gritted his teeth. "Not gonna happen, Zee. I won't let it."

She slumped back in the booth, and he mentally prepared to deliver the speech he'd prepared on his twenty-five-hour drive from Lagniappe. He rubbed his scratchy eyes, wondering if he ought to wait until he'd slept to launch into this discussion.

The very real possibility that she'd hate his idea and turn it down stirred a drumbeat of caution in his chest. The last time they'd taken their friendship in a new direction, he'd nearly lost her. Her rejection had cut a wide, deep swath that still ached on days like today. The plan he'd devised was risky, but he'd take the chance of getting hurt again if it would help Zoey.

He'd do anything for Zee, even put his heart on the line.

"Aren't you going to eat?" she asked, nodding toward his half-eaten pizza. The other half sat like a rock in his gut.

"I'm not hungry. I ate earlier." Gage shoved his napkin under the edge of his plate and took a deep breath. "I have an idea, but before you answer me, I want you to hear me out. Okay?"

She wrinkled her nose as she munched a French fry, a mannerism he remembered from high school that meant she was skeptical but curious. "Okay. What?"

He pressed his palms on the table and met her gaze. Her bright jade eyes held such open trust and affection that he almost balked. What if he screwed this up and she got hurt?

"I've been thinking about your situation—and mine—and I think we can help each other."

More nose scrunching. "Help each other how?"

"What if there was a way for you to go back to Lagniappe and face your family with your head high and your future secure?"

She arched a copper eyebrow and propped her elbows on the table. "I'm listening."

"I need help with Pet."

"Pet?"

"Elaine's daughter. I told you about her, right?"

Zoey tipped her head. "Yeah. I thought her name was Magnolia or something."

"Petunia. We call her Pet because Petunia is just…well, a ridiculous name. I have custody of her while Elaine deals with her alcohol problem."

Zoey's eyes widened. "You're raising a baby? By yourself? Since when?"

"Well, she's not a baby anymore. She's five, but she's still a handful. And yes, I'm doing it alone—well, except for the babysitter who watches her while I'm at the fire station. I've had Pet since August, so…about a month now."

Zoey flopped back in the booth, grinning broadly. "You're a father!"

He raised a hand and shook his head. "I'm an uncle just trying to help out."

"Gage, that's so…awesome. If I said I was proud of you, would you take it the right way? 'Cause you must be the best brother *ever* to raise Pet for Elaine."

He held up a hand. "This isn't permanent. Just until Elaine gets her act together and can be the parent she should be."

Combing her thick hair back from her face, Zoey shook her head. "Like that will ever happen. Elaine's way too much like your mom. I'd be surprised if she ever gets her life in any shape to take care of a kid. Not without serious counseling."

Gage's gut tightened. Zoey's brutal honesty cut close to the truth. She'd seen his family, up close and personal, throughout high school. After Zoey had nursed Gage's injuries from one of his dad's beatings in eighth grade, he'd seen no point in hiding the ugly truth from her. His family put the *dys* in dysfunctional. His parents might be gone now—his mother succumbing to illness right after he finished high school, his father killed in a car-versus-tree wreck just last year—but their warped legacy lived on. Zoey's family, the hours, days, weeks he'd taken refuge in their pool house, had been his saving grace throughout his troubled youth.

Gage cleared his throat. "Yeah, well…that's why Elaine's in a clinic now, drying out. We'll see if it sticks."

"Okay, so back to your idea. This will save

my pride, give me a future, give you help with Pet and—" She grinned. "What, cure cancer? How do you figure to do all that?"

Gage reached into his jacket pocket and pulled out the small box he'd brought with him from home.

Lifting the lid on the jewelry box, he showed her the small emerald ring. Emerald to match her eyes. What a sap he was.

Zoey goggled at the ring. "Leapin' lizards! Gage?"

"So we're in Vegas, right? Marry me, Zee."

Chapter 3

Nervous jitters danced down Zoey's spine, and she popped up from the chair in the waiting area of the I Do, I Do Wedding Chapel to pace. All of Gage's reasoning sounded good in theory, but the reality of marrying Gage still left Zoey off balance. Wary. *Terrified.*

And her inability to quit staring at his five-o'clock-shadowed jaw line and buff fireman's build left her just...confused. And flush-faced.

"Just so we're straight on this," she said, aiming a finger at her groom, who looked a little pale around the gills himself, "this isn't permanent. When we both have our lives back on track—after my baby comes and I have a job, and when Elaine takes custody of Pet again—we get a simple divorce and go our separate ways, no hard feelings, no complications. Right?"

Gage's jaw tightened, and his nostrils flared as he sucked in a deep breath. "Right."

She paced across the room and back, acid building in her stomach as she found the courage to lay out her number-one rule. She wet her lips and squeezed her hands into fists to stop them from shaking. "And no sex. This isn't *really* a marriage, and...well, we know how sex messed things up for us last time."

His eyes darkened, and his gaze narrowed. He said nothing, but she knew he was remembering the last time, the *only* time they'd slept together...and the morning after.

The night of graduation filtered through her mind like an apparition, haunting her. She could still hear the cheers of her classmates as they tossed their caps, could still smell the beer and "jungle juice" Marty Haines served at his postgraduation party. But most vividly, she remembered looking for Gage, not seeing him at the party, but finding him later, waiting for her at her family's pool house. With a black eye.

Though she'd been tipsy, she'd let him vent about his father, offered him comfort and...one thing had led to another. Zoey had compounded the drunken mistake of sleeping with her best friend with her impulsive gut reaction the next morning. In a panic and without a word to Gage, she'd fled Lagniappe for Europe—a decision that had nearly ruined their friendship.

"No sex," she repeated. "We can't repeat that mistake. Our friendship is more important than a night of doing the mattress tango." She pressed a hand to her swirling stomach. "Agreed?"

Gage held her gaze, his dark stare unnerving. He cracked his knuckles, a sure sign that he wasn't as cool and collected inside as his relaxed manner suggested. Finally, he turned a hand up in concession. "Fine. No sex. But we still respect our wedding vows. No infidelity."

She jerked a nod. *"Naturellement."*

His scowl reminded her how much he hated

her speaking French, a too-raw reminder of her years away "finding herself" in Europe.

"But to keep the divorce simple, I think we should—"

Gage growled and surged to his feet. "Can we *not* plan every detail of our divorce now? It's bad enough you've talked about nothing but how this won't be a 'real' marriage—" glowering, he made quotation marks in the air with his fingers "—since the minute you put on my engagement ring. If you don't want to marry me, just say so. Otherwise, can we try to be at least a *little* optimistic before we walk down the aisle?"

"Easy, Sparky." She stepped up to him and patted his chest. His broad, hard, well-developed chest. She let her hand linger longer than she should have, and he arched an eyebrow. *Leapin' lizards.* "I just want to make sure we're on the same page before we say 'I do.'"

She savored the warmth of his skin that seeped through his shirt and felt the reassuring thump of his heart under her hand. Strong and steady, just like Gage. Reminded of all he'd sacrificed to help her, Zoey cupped his cheek with her hand. His unshaven jaw scratched her hand, and she marveled again at the changes in him since high school. Who was this calendar-worthy hottie she was about to marry? Sure, she'd seen him since graduation. Dozens of times. But in her mind, Gage would always be the quiet, skinny boy who didn't shave until his junior year. The lanky track-team distance runner. The geeky guy no one noticed and whose name was misspelled "Gabe" in the senior yearbook.

But women noticed him now. At the restaurant alone, she'd counted five different women who'd looked ready to jump him if he'd shown even a hint of interest. Her best friend, the late bloomer, the fireman hunk. Who'da thunk it?

"Thanks again for coming to my rescue. Now I don't have to go home to face my parents unwed, penniless, pregnant and deserted." She quirked a wry grin. "Just penniless and pregnant."

He shrugged. As if driving fifteen hundred miles without sleeping, as if putting his life on hold so her baby would have a name, as if saving her from being homeless were nothing.

He wrapped his fingers around hers and moved them from his cheek to brush a soft kiss across her knuckles. A sensation like tiny bubbles tickled down her spine.

"What are friends for? I wouldn't have survived high school if not for you and your family. Consider this payback."

The doors to the chapel opened, and a man wearing a sparkly suit that Liberace would envy called, "Powell-Bancroft?"

Gage and Zoey looked from Mr. Sparkles to each other. She saw the get-a-load-of-*him* grin Gage fought to hide and had to bite the inside of her own cheek so she wouldn't laugh. "Are you sure this is the wedding chapel and not the *Salute to Siegfried and Roy?*" she whispered.

Gage's cheek twitched, and his gaze lit with humor. "Just in case, keep an eye out for tigers in there, okay?" He offered her his arm. "Shall we?"

Her stomach swirled, and her burger-and-fries lunch rebelled. "Is this the right thing to do, Gage? I mean, the last thing I want is to do anything that will hurt our friendship."

His dark eyebrows lowered, his expression cautious. "I'm sure. I thought about all the pros and cons driving out here. But if you're not sure, if you need more time to think—"

"That would be so *not* me. Right?" She raked her hair back with her fingers and gave him a nervous laugh. "Impulsive is my middle name. Isn't that what my mother says?" She hooked her arm in his and squared her shoulders. "Let's do this."

A tinny organ played the Wagner wedding march, and Zoey squeezed Gage's hand as they strode down the aisle to the vaudevillesque minister. Her stomach seesawed, her lip sweated and her knees trembled. This was hardly how she pictured her wedding day as a little girl.

She swallowed hard, forcing down the bile that rose in her throat when the minister, a show-perfect smile in place, intoned, "We're gathered here today to join Zoey and Gabe—"

"Gage," her groom corrected.

The pearly-white smile faltered. "Oh,

uh...Zoey and Gage in the legal bonds of marriage."

Her heart thundered, and she thought she might throw up. Maybe the hot peppers on her burger had been a mistake...but she'd had a strange craving for them and—

"Zoey, do you take Gage to be your husband? To love and cherish in sickness and—" The minister's voice faded to a drone as she faced her groom. Her *groom*. Leapin' lizards! She'd spent her whole life making rash decisions, screwing up, hurting the people she loved. How could she live with herself if, in trying to dig herself out of the hole she'd created with Derek, she was making matters worse by marrying Gage?

She was ready to turn and run when she met Gage's eyes. Warm, genuine, encouraging. He flashed her one of his crooked grins and, as if David Copperfield had waved his hands and snatched away a silky veil, her jitters vanished. *Poof!* Gage had been her rock, her refuge, her home base for more than eleven years. With him, she was safe, anchored.

"—until death do you part?" the showman minister finished grandly.

A niggle of guilt poked her. Their marriage would be temporary, not until death, but the confidence in Gage's eyes filled her with a calm assurance she was doing the right thing. Warmth filled her chest. "Yeah, I do."

Relief to have her vows over with buzzed through Zoey as the Liberace double repeated the vows for Gage. In response, Gage's expression warmed. "Absolutely, positively."

Zoey quirked an eyebrow. His answer seemed over-the-top, when a simple "I do" would have sufficed. But maybe Gage was getting caught up in the whole Las Vegas flash and dazzle. Or maybe he was trying to make her laugh at the absurdity of their tying the knot in Vegas like something from an episode of *Friends*. He surprised her again by producing from his pocket a plain band to slip on her finger at the appointed time. When she gave him a curious look, he only winked and turned to face the minister. They signed the marriage license to make it official, and the tinny organ tuned up again with "Going to the Chapel of Love."

The minister gave Gage a sly grin. "You can kiss her now."

Zoey sputtered, heat creeping to her cheeks. "Naw. See, we're not really—"

Gage caught her wrist and reeled her close with a firm tug. "You heard the man, Zee. Shut up and kiss me."

Her stomach swooped in anticipation. To cover, she pulled a face and buzzed her lips in dismissal. "Yeah, right. We're not—"

Capturing her nape with one hand, Gage anchored her against his long, lean body with his other arm. He silenced her startled gasp with a kiss that was far from platonic. His warm mouth covered hers, drawing on it with gentle but insistent persuasion. Zoey clutched at his T-shirt to steady herself as his tongue traced the seam of her lips and her head spun dizzily. A sensation like hot maple syrup flowed through her veins, sweet and indulgent, while Gage's skillful lips teased and tantalized hers. Around her, the chapel lost focus, and the organ was drowned out by the whoosh of blood in her ears.

When he angled his head to deepen the kiss, she surrendered to the heady pleasure that swamped her and answered the tug of his mouth with her own fervor. Gage massaged her neck with his fingers, his caress seductive and hypnotizing. Heat and need coiled low in her belly as she melted into him. His kiss was commanding yet tender, powerful, romantic—and unexpectedly erotic.

When he backed away, leaving her shaking and breathless, Gage's grin was cocky, his dark eyes on fire. "And don't you forget it."

Weak-kneed, she blinked at him—stunned, confused…and aroused. Aroused by *Gage?* What was happening to her?

"Leapin' lizards," she rasped, touching her fingers to her lips, half expecting to find them ablaze. "What was *that?*"

"That, Mrs. Powell—" Gage took a step back, rolled his shoulders and twisted his mouth in regret "—is just a taste of what you'll be missing." He laced their fingers and nudged her down the aisle with her arm tucked under his. Giving her a side glance, he arched an eyebrow. "So…how do you feel about your no-sex rule now?"

Gage loaded the last of Zoey's belongings into the back of his Ford Escape—or rather Elaine's Escape. He was using the SUV while his sister was in rehab and he had Pet. He slammed the back end of the vehicle closed and glanced up to the door of the motel room where Zoey emerged with her purse and a backpack. Having never officially checked out, due to her lack of funds, Zoey was still technically renting the room. So they'd returned long enough for Gage to get a shower and a nap before hitting the road.

She'd been unusually quiet since the wedding ceremony, and Gage mentally kicked himself for kissing her so passionately. A chaste kiss to seal the union would have been enough. Or no kiss, as Zoey had wanted, would have been safest. But all her talk about how their marriage wouldn't be real, how they couldn't have sex, how sleeping together their only time had been a mistake had frustrated him.

And, yeah, he knew that harboring any hope that living as man and wife, sharing the same roof, renewing the bonds that had made them so close in high school would eventually change her feelings for him was a recipe for disaster and heartache. But maybe a little of Zoey's recklessness had rubbed off on him because, damn it, he still clung to the shred of hope that someday Zoey would see what she meant to him and return his feelings. The kiss at the I Do, I Do Wedding Chapel just demonstrated that they had chemistry beyond friendship. His body temperature rose just remembering the heat in Zoey's kiss. The way her raspberry lips had parted in surprise and a pink blush had crept over her cheeks. She'd made a beautiful bride.

For whatever reason, Zoey was scared to recognize that attraction and embrace it. He'd known that ever since he woke up alone the morning after graduation. Kissing her today had been stupid. He couldn't push her, or he risked having her run from him again as she had six years ago. He couldn't risk hurting her while she was vulnerable, couldn't risk frightening her away when she was still reeling from Derek's desertion. She needed him to be her friend while she dealt with the mess she was in and got her feet under her again.

Gage dragged a hand down his face and sighed. *Patience, buddy. Just have patience.*

Yet another small voice, an echo from the past, whispered to him, *You're a dope if you think she'll ever want you. She's going to run again. She's going to hurt you. That's who she is and what she does. You can't change her.*

"I think that's everything." Zoey opened a back door and tossed in her backpack. "Did you pay the motel manager?"

Gage shoved his hands in the back pockets of his jeans. "Yeah. We're good to go."

Zoey gnawed her bottom lip. "I'm going to pay you back. All of it. I hate that you got stuck settling my debts."

"Forget it."

She frowned. "Never. I'm gonna pay you back. I *am*."

"Zoey?" The voice came from behind Gage, and even before he turned, he saw Zoey's expression and knew who it was.

"What the hell are you doing here, Derek?" Her tone was brittle, hurt.

Gage bristled and stepped in front of Derek when he tried to approach Zoey. "Beat it, dude. She doesn't want to talk to you."

Derek ignored Gage and leaned sideways to see past him. "I just want a minute, Red. We gotta talk."

"I have nothing to say to you." She snatched open the passenger door of the Escape and dropped her purse on the seat. "Ready, Gage?"

"Gage?" Derek cocked his head and studied him. "You're her friend from school."

Squaring his shoulders, Gage narrowed a defensive glare on the man who'd used Zoey and discarded her like yesterday's news. "Actually, I'm her husband now. And I'm taking her home. So beat it."

Derek's eyebrows shot up, and he coughed a

laugh. "Her husband? You know she's pregnant, right?"

Gage's blood pressure spiked, and he balled his fists. "Yeah, I know," he growled through gritted teeth. "And I know you weren't man enough to take responsibility for your baby. But I care about Zoey, and I will protect her from you and anyone else who tries to hurt her or her baby."

Derek raised his hands. "Easy, man, I don't want to hurt her. I just gotta talk to her." Turning toward Zoey again, his expression turned beseeching and somewhat desperate. "If you're married now and going home, then you must have access to some money again. I need your help, Red. Please."

She scoffed. "Get real."

"C'mon, Zoey. Viper's breathing down my neck. I gotta get him his money soon or things could get ugly."

She pointed to her bruised eye. "They already got ugly. Viper tried to squeeze the money from me. But I'm done being your ATM. Haven't you stolen enough from me?"

Derek sidled around Gage and approached Zoey. "You can't do this to me, Zoey! I need that money. Do it for what we had." He paused and got a gleam in his eye. "Do it for our kid."

She stiffened. "You lost any right to speak of *our* baby when you told me not to keep it!"

"I'm sorry about that. Really. I just panicked." He paused and hung his head, turning his palms up in a pleading gesture. "Please, I just need a little cash."

"What you need is professional help. You're a gambling addict, Derek." Whirling away, she slid into the front seat and slammed the Escape's door. Gage took his cue and headed toward the driver's side, but when Derek jerked Zoey's door open to confront her again, he detoured.

"Please, Zoey. I need money! I'll get help. I will, but please, don't do this…"

Gage grabbed the back of Derek's shirt and hauled him away from Zoey. He could smell the desperation that rolled off Derek in waves. Pitiful. With a firm thrust, he shoved Derek to the pavement. "I'm warning you, if you ever come near her again or try to steal money from her in any way, I will hurt you worse than any loan shark ever could."

Without looking back, Gage stormed around the front fender and climbed behind the wheel. Protective rage seethed inside him as he gunned the engine.

Derek staggered to his feet and smacked the side of the SUV as Gage peeled out of the motel parking lot. "You haven't heard the last of me, Red! You owe me!"

In the passenger seat, Zoey shuddered and squeezed her eyes shut. Gage wrapped his hand around the fist she balled in her lap. "I won't let him hurt you, Zee. I swear it."

She cast a green-eyed glance at him, full of trust, apology and appreciation, and his heart kicked. He'd keep his promise to protect Zoey and her baby, no matter what. And somehow he'd find a way to guard his heart.

Chapter 4

Standing on her parents' front porch, Zoey drew a deep breath, shelved her pride. She mustered the nerve to face her father's I-told-you-sos and the crestfallen disapproval in her mother's eyes. Gage reassured her with a gentle shoulder squeeze that stirred warmth in her belly. Although glad to have him beside her, bolstering her courage, this was her battle, her mess to clean up, and she couldn't rely on him to be her knight this time, swooping in to save her from her parents' disenchantment.

Within seconds of Zoey's firm knock on the

massive mahogany door, her mother answered the summons, her face reflecting first shock, then joy, before the first hints of suspicion and concern etched creases around her eyes. "Zoey! Honey...I— What—?"

Her mother clapped a hand to her chest as if trying to catch her breath. Ellen Bancroft's gaze darted to Gage before returning to her prodigal daughter.

"Surprise." Zoey forced a grin, her heart tap-dancing in her chest. "I'm home and...I have news. Is Dad around?"

"Yes, somewhere. Come in." Her mother ushered them inside, greeting Gage with a hug.

"Neil, it's Zoey and Gage! Where are you?" Ellen called toward the kitchen, then waved them toward the family room couch.

On the mantel, Zoey spotted the newest framed pictures in her parents' collection. Wedding pictures for both of her older sisters, a family shot of Holly with her husband and her new stepchildren, and a cameo of Paige and her husband, Jake, at the ribbon cutting of their new private security firm. A twinge of jealousy nipped at her. Her sisters had success, family, careers...a multitude of reasons their parents could be proud. Zoey's picture was conspicuously missing. But, then, what had she done lately that was memorable or photo-worthy?

Sibling rivalry was nothing new to her. She'd long been falling short of her sisters' high-water marks. She'd learned early in life that she didn't have the good grades and ambition that earned praise for Paige or the good behavior and sweet disposition that garnered Holly their parents' endearments. She'd fought her restless nature, struggled to make passing grades, but her adventurous impulses continually led her into mischief and her parents' bad graces.

Then in junior high, she'd discovered drama club. She could be melodramatic, loud and over-the-top, and people approved. She could pretend to be someone else, and her family applauded. She'd found her niche in acting, a way to live her life in bold gestures and big emotions, and her family didn't roll their eyes in frustration or shake their heads in dismay.

But when high school ended, so had her acting

career. She'd abandoned the stage in pursuit of new adventures—Europe after graduation. A half-dozen attempts to find a career that had a brighter future than that of starving actor. Then Derek.

The thud of footsteps on the hardwood hall floor preceded Neil Bancroft's appearance at the study door. When he spotted Zoey, he stilled, stared, then crossed the room in three giant steps to fold his daughter in a warm embrace. "Welcome home, sweetheart. Are you all right?"

Zoey's throat tightened with emotion. She hadn't expected her father's affectionate greeting, considering the acrimony of their last conversation in this room. Still pressed against her father's chest, she nodded, not trusting her voice. Finally, Neil stepped back, squaring his shoulders. Shaking from her rioting emotions, Zoey sank onto the couch next to her husband. *Her husband.* Leapin' lizards.

Gage rose long enough to shake Neil's hand in greeting. Her father nodded a welcome before casting a quick look around the room. "Is *he* here, too?"

Her father's tone of voice, his derogatory emphasis, left no question of whom he meant. Zoey bristled at her father's shift into a combative demeanor, and Gage, clearly reading her body language, placed a hand on her knee, silently advising patience. The warmth of his hand seeped through her jeans and stirred a giddy flutter in her belly. The memory of their wedding kiss teased the edges of her thoughts, rattling her further. Why did Gage have this unnerving effect on her now? Was it just because they were married? Biting her lip, she fumbled for composure before answering her father. "No. He...we broke up."

She divided a glance between her parents, gauging their reaction to this news. Her father arched a graying eyebrow, indicating he expected an explanation, while her mother's expression lit with hope and relief. Beside the couch where Zoey perched, a large grandfather clock stood sentinel over the room, while its ticktocking reverberated in the ensuing quiet like a game-show timer, urging her to continue.

Her father crossed his arms and cocked his head. "How much did he take you for?"

His confidence in his question chafed. Zoey raised her chin, vacillating between, "Who says he took me for anything?" and the truth. But what good would denials do, other than salve her pride for a few seconds before she came clean?

She rubbed her palms on her jeans and huffed a sigh. "Everything."

Her mother gasped. Her father groaned. Gage wrapped his hand around hers and squeezed. The gesture, in the face of her parents' obvious dismay and disappointment in her, was like landing in an unexpected safety net after a ten-story fall.

I'm here. I stand with you. I care. His unspoken support brought tears to her eyes.

Neil Bancroft narrowed his eyes and frowned. "Your savings?"

She nodded.

"Your inheritance?"

More tears prickled her eyes. Shame was a bitter pill. "Everything."

"Criminy, Zoey!" Neil shoved a hand through his silver hair. "I *knew* this would happen. I told you he was—"

"A jerk and a loser and a freeloader, and I didn't listen because I was in love." Zoey shoved to her feet, raising her voice to be heard over her father's. "I know. You were right, and I screwed up. Again. I'm a disappointment to the family, and the worst daughter ever. Does that about cover it?"

"No, honey! Don't say that." Her mother rushed over to her, placing herself between her husband and daughter. "You're a wonderful daughter, and we love you."

"What about your stock in the company? Your shares of Bancroft Industries?"

"Neil!" Ellen sent her husband a quelling look.

But Zoey's spirits lifted. She'd forgotten her stake in the family business, small though it was. Derek hadn't gotten everything. "No." Relief filled her tone. Her smile welled from inside her, and she turned to Gage before answering her father. "I still have my stock."

Her father dragged a hand over his face as he stalked to a wingback chair and sat down. "Well, that's something anyway."

Her mother gave her father another scolding look, then turned to Zoey with a stiff smile. "You said you had news. Good news?"

The hopeful tone of her mother's question, as if she didn't really expect good news and was bracing for the worst, raked through Zoey. Not that she could blame her mom. Zoey had more often than not been the bearer of bad news. She'd gotten detention for cutting class. She'd maxed out her credit card. She wasn't going to college. She'd gotten arrested at an environmental group's protest rally and needed to be bailed out of jail.

Yeah, she'd dropped a few bombs in her day. And today's missile had an atomic warhead.

"Um, well…" When she hedged, Gage shoved to his feet and slid an arm around her shoulders, pulling her close. The press of his hard body against hers brought a flush to her skin from her scalp to her toes.

"Yes. Good news. Very good news." His voice was strong, confident and happy. He gave her a side glance that said *Trust me.*

Her father raised his eyebrow. *Go on.*

Her mother leaned forward, her expression eager.

Zoey opened her mouth, then closed it, the words stuck in her throat. *I'm pregnant.*

When she faltered, Gage jumped in again. "We're married." She could hear a smile in his voice as he made the announcement, and Zoey's heart tripped.

Her parents stared, mouths gaping.

"It was an impromptu thing, but heartfelt," he continued. "I've been waiting ten years for her to say yes, so when she did, I didn't waste time and give her the chance to back out."

Shock gave way to joy on her mother's face, and her father sat back in his chair nodding his approval. And why not? Gage had always been like a son to them, thanks to his many hours with the family, his place at the table for holiday meals, his help with yard work, repairs and washing dishes. When each of his parents died, her parents had anonymously paid for the funerals, though Gage had figured out easily enough who'd made the generous gesture.

Gage stroked his hand from her shoulder to her arm and hugged her to his side, beaming, playing his part as a newlywed to a T. Apparently, he should have been on the stage instead of working on the sets during high school. The guy had a hidden acting talent, currently out in force. Zoey almost believed that he was really as blissful as he pretended about their I'm-saving-your-ass, not-really-real marriage of convenience. And like a lust-crazed honeymooner's, her nerve endings crackled in response to his tender touch, and a hum of desire coiled in her belly.

Although distracted by her reaction to Gage, she summoned a bit of her own thespian talent and flashed a smile to her parents. "And…" She paused for dramatic effect as if she were spilling the best part, instead of the catch. "We're expecting. I'm pregnant."

The shock returned. More gaping.

Zoey's cheeks felt leaden as she tried to hold her smile in place. "I'm due in April."

Ellen pressed her hand to her mouth. "Oh, Zoey, Gage, congratulations! I'm so happy for you." She stepped up to them and drew them both into a group hug. "This is such a surprise... except not really. I always had a feeling you two might end up together. Oh!" Her mother laughed and kissed Gage's cheek. "Welcome to the family, honey."

Zoey peered around Gage as her mother hugged him again, and they exchanged more pleasantries. Her father hadn't said anything yet, and his gaze was directed toward the floor.

His expression boded ill. He didn't appear mad exactly. More confused, skeptical.

She swallowed hard. Oh, Lord. He was doing the math. When he met her gaze, Zoey knew she was busted.

"The baby isn't Gage's, is it?"

Her mother and Gage fell silent, turning toward Neil when he spoke. Zoey's heart thumped. She said nothing.

"It's Derek's baby. Am I right?" Her father's expression sagged with disenchantment.

Zoey raised her chin, working to keep her hurt and frustration from coloring her tone. But failing. "It's *my* baby. That's what matters."

"And *that's* why Gage married you," he spoke softly, but his tone radioed his disillusionment. "Because you were pregnant, and Derek had dumped you."

"Maybe *I* dumped *Derek*." Semantics, she knew, but Zoey felt compelled to put a more positive spin on the matter. "What matters is I saw his true stripes, and he's out of my life."

Or so she hoped. She could still hear the desperation in his voice as she and Gage drove away from the Vegas motel. *You haven't heard the last of me, Red! You owe me!*

She suppressed a shudder. It would be just like Derek to haunt her life the way the acrid scent of his cigarettes clung to her clothes.

"So Gage only married you to save your reputation and give your baby a n—"

"Actually, sir," Gage interrupted, his voice firm. "I married Zoey for the reasons I gave earlier. I care for Zoey and always have. I *wanted* to marry her."

Zoey's heart pattered with a bittersweet ache. Her hero. Rescuing her from her father's condemnation. He really was putting on quite a good show for her parents' sake. She studied the firm set of his mouth and marveled again at the changes in him, the rugged appeal of his square jaw and harsh cheekbones.

"And you don't have a problem with raising another man's baby?" Her father seemed shocked, suspicious. "Do you have any idea how much a baby costs? You understand she has no savings anymore. The burden of paying for this baby will fall to you, son."

"My friendship with Zoey has never had anything to do with money, how much she had or didn't have. And I'm sure I will love her baby as if it were my own. Just like Zoey will care for my niece with genuine affection."

Appreciation for Gage's defense of her warmed Zoey's heart, but guilt sliced through her in its wake. This was her mess. She couldn't let Gage fall on the sword for her. She had to stand up to her father's chastisement, take the blame for her mistakes and take responsibility for turning her life around. Starting with facing the truth and not hiding behind a sham marriage.

"Your niece?" Her father cocked his eyebrow in his do-tell way again.

Enough. She stepped forward, squaring her shoulders as she faced her father. "Okay, yes. The baby is Derek's. I realize that I've let you down." Her voice cracked, and she slapped a hand to her chest. "I've let *me* down. I have no reason to expect you to be happy about my circumstances, but Gage was willing to sacrifice everything to help me." She raised her chin and leveled a steady gaze on her father. "So don't judge Gage or his choices. He's doing this all for me, and I love him for it."

She felt Gage stiffen beside her, sensed more than saw the startled glance he shot toward her. "And yes, our marriage is more of a business arrangement than a love match." She heard Gage sigh, saw her mother deflate, recognized the resignation in her father's face. Pain plucked at her, knowing how she'd failed her parents and what her mistakes had cost Gage. Clearing the clog of emotion from her throat, she explained the symbiotic arrangement she and Gage had agreed upon. "When the time comes, we've agreed to a quiet...divorce." A vise squeezed her chest so tightly that she could barely rasp the last word.

A heavy silence fell over the room, and tears stung her sinuses. Maybe coming back to Lagniappe had been a mistake. Maybe her parents would have been better off if she'd stayed away, let them think she was still happily living the life of a gypsy with her poker-playing boyfriend. Maybe accepting Gage's proposal had been another selfish mistake that would come back to haunt her and break his heart. Even the thought of hurting him made her lungs ache until she couldn't breathe.

She flipped her hair over her shoulder and stood taller. Too late for second-guessing. All she could do now was plow forward and do everything in her power to avoid making things worse or hurting anyone she loved any further with additional screwups.

"I'm sorry." She heard the tremble in her voice and cleared her throat before she continued. "I know that's not what you wanted to hear, but you deserved the truth."

Gage pressed his mouth in a hard line of disappointment.

She tipped her head and mouthed, "What?"

He shook his head and turned his attention to the window.

"Zoey—" Her father scratched his cheek and sighed his frustration. "Marriage is not something to be taken lightly. It's not supposed to be a business arrangement."

"Sure it is," she countered. "For centuries marriages were arranged for political, business and social reasons. The concept of marriage as a love match is really a rather modern concept."

Her father grunted. "Why do you have to be so argumentative? So exasperating?"

Ellen leaned forward, jumping into the fray. "Maybe, given some time, you'll decide that you want to stay married to Gage." Her mother paused and divided a look between Zoey and Gage. "Maybe living together as husband and wife, you two will fall in love. You know, the best marriages are based on friendship."

The note of forced cheer and optimism in her mother's voice stirred a bittersweet longing inside Zoey. But she couldn't dwell on longings and selfish wants anymore. She'd been chasing her dreams for years, leaving a trail of disappointment and heartache in her path. Time to sacrifice what she wanted to make sure no one else got hurt.

Her father took a deep breath and gave the two of them a thoughtful look. "Zoey, my father always told me that life is ten percent what happens to you and ninety percent how you respond to what happens. I hope you gave this decision careful consideration."

She swallowed hard. Did thirty minutes as they found a wedding chapel count as careful consideration? Somehow she doubted her father would think so.

Gage slid a hand to the small of her back and nudged her toward the door. "If you're ready, Zee, my niece has been with the babysitter for four days. We need to get home and relieve the poor gal from Pet patrol."

Zoey's mother rose and gave her a tight hug. "We'll talk soon, okay? With a baby coming, there is so much to plan! Have you told your sisters about your marriage and the baby?"

Zoey's spirits lifted. *Holly and Paige.* Next to Gage, her sisters were her best friends. But how would they react to her news?

"Not yet. We wanted you to be the first to know." And she'd known if she told her sisters, her parents might have found out before she could break the news.

As they made their way to the front door, she promised to be in touch with her mother before the end of the week, shared a wisecrack with Gage about the meter running on the babysitter and monitored her father's brooding silence.

Make the first move, her conscience nudged her while the stubborn brat in her balked.

Gage opened the front door and stood aside for her to exit first. She took a step toward the porch, then hesitated when guilt kicked her in the shin.

"Dad—"

"Zoey—" he said at the same time, and they chuckled awkwardly.

She rushed over to her father and threw her arms around his neck, like she had every night as a child when he'd walk through the door at the end of a long business day.

"I love you, Baby Bear," he murmured as he squeezed her to his chest.

The moniker took her back twenty years to nights when her favorite bedtime event was acting out Goldilocks with her father and sisters. Blonde Holly was Goldilocks, and Paige was Mama Bear, but the most dramatic and heartfelt performance each night belonged to Zoey.

Tears puddled in her eyes and, from a throat tight with emotion, she squeaked, "I love you, too, Papa Bear."

Gage glanced across the front seat at Zoey, who was chewing a fingernail with a vengeance. "Haven't kicked that bad habit yet, eh, Zee?"

She paused and stared at her finger as if she hadn't realized what she was doing until he called it to her attention. With an annoyed twist of her lips, she sat on her hands and pressed her lips into a taut line.

He tapped his thumbs on the steering wheel. "So...that went pretty well, doncha think?"

She wrinkled her nose. "Were you not in the same room with us? They hate me now."

Gage nodded. "Oh...so *that's* what 'I love you, Baby Bear' means. It was code for 'I hate my daughter.' I was wondering about that." Remembering the lingering hug the father and daughter had shared stirred a familiar longing in Gage. He'd always envied Zoey for the family she had, the love and support. The obvious affection Zoey's father had for her was so starkly different from the animosity and indifference he'd grown up with.

She scoffed. "You know what I mean. I've failed them, and they're hurt and disappointed and disillusioned and disgusted and angry and—"

"Yeah. Maybe. Understandably so. Did you really expect anything else?"

Sighing, she pulled a hand out and nibbled a cuticle. "No."

"They'll get over it." He reached over and caught her hand in his, pulling it away from her mouth. "The important thing is they love you. They're glad to have you back home and want to see you turn things around."

"Maybe."

"Definitely."

Zoey tucked her hand under her leg again and rocked her head from side to side stretching her muscles. The gesture drew his attention to the smooth ivory arch of her neck, and he squelched the urge to press his lips to the pulse point under her jaw and inhale the fruity aroma of her shampoo.

Gage made the turn into his neighborhood, and he glanced at Zoey to gauge her reaction to the modest homes along the street. His house was a far cry from the dumpy trailer he'd grown up in, but what would Zoey think of it? She'd led a life of privilege with her parents well beyond his firefighter's salary. "So this is it," he said, pulling into his driveway. "Home sweet home."

A smile tugged her sensuous lips when she faced him, and it was all he could do to not steal a kiss. "I like. Did you plant the pansies by the porch?"

He cut the engine. "Not really. I bought them already in the pots at Rani's urging."

Her eyebrow lifted in a way reminiscent of her father's mannerism. "Rani?"

"My babysitter. She claimed my yard needed some fall color." He hitched his head toward the house. "She's inside. Come meet her."

He turned to open his car door, but Zoey stopped him with a hand on his shoulder.

"Gage, thank you. For defending me to my dad. You didn't have to say all that stuff about how you wanted to marry me and all." She puffed one cheek out as she sighed and rolled her eyes. "I appreciate your putting a positive spin on things with your ain't-this-great-news shtick."

A heaviness settled in his chest. She'd thought he was feeding her father a line to cover for her.

More evidence that she viewed their arrangement from a far different perspective than he did. As if her frankness with her parents, calling their marriage a business arrangement that would eventually end in divorce, weren't enough to prove that point.

Sirens in his head blared, "Warning, Will Robinson!" He definitely needed to reel in his feelings and expectations or he was headed for another disaster with Zoey. One that could kill their friendship for good. His hand tightened on the door handle. "You're welcome, but…I said it because I meant it. I'm glad you're here."

Angling her head, she gave him a gooey-eyed look. "You're the sweetest. I didn't mean to sound like I have a problem with this arrangement. I'm looking forward to spending time with you. Catching up. Rebuilding our friendship."

Friendship. The word landed in his gut like a brick.

Hello, Powell, can I paint you a picture? She only wants to be friends.

He forced a half grin. "Okay, then. Are you ready to meet the monster?"

She chuckled. "The monster?"

"Pet. She's precious, and I love her, but she reminds me at times of Stitch."

"What?" Zoey's laughter bubbled through him with the effect of champagne on an empty stomach. Warming, intoxicating…

"You know, the alien from that Disney movie? A movie she loves to watch, by the way."

"I know who Stitch is. I just can't believe a little girl could be that bad."

Gage popped open his door. "My sister gave Pet little, if any, structure for the last five years, so…believe it. You've been warned."

He climbed out of the SUV and hauled Zoey's bags from the rear cargo space before heading inside.

"We're home!" he called into the house where the scent of grilled cheese and the whimsical sounds of a cartoon wafted in from the back room.

"Uncle Gage!" Pet came charging in and tackled his legs, nearly knocking him over.

He caught her under her arms and swung her up. "Hey, Squirt. Were you good for Rani?"

"Rrrowr," Pet growled, curling her fingers into faux-claws.

"I was afraid of that." He nodded toward Zoey. "Pet, remember I told you before my trip that I had to go help a friend? This is Zoey. She's going to be living with us. She's my wife now, which makes her your aunt."

Pet eyed Zoey warily. "Is an aunt like a stepmother? In my cartoons, the stepmother is always mean."

Zoey grinned. "Then you're watching the wrong cartoons because all the stepmothers I know are really nice. And aunts are even better. Aunts are fun."

Pet's eyes brightened, and she looked to him for confirmation.

Gage nodded. "Yep, you and Zoey can have lots of fun together."

"Hey, Mr. Gage. How was the trip?" Rani Ogatini, a college student with the patience of a saint and an obvious love for young children, strolled in from the kitchen.

"Successful. Rani, this is Zoey Ban—er, Zoey Powell. My new wife."

His use of his last name clearly startled Zoey, who blinked at him before shaking hands with Rani and offering a bright smile.

"So you're Gage's monster wrangler?" Zoey asked after the traditional pleasantries and congratulations on their wedding had been exchanged. The sweep of his bride's gaze clearly sized up the attractive coed even as she made nice.

Rani gave her a wry grin. "Aw, Pet's not that bad. She's just got a lot of energy and a wild imagination."

Gage scoffed. "You say tom-A-to, I say to-MAH-to. Seems to me she's on a mission to find the most unusual way to end up in the emergency room at the most inconvenient hour possible." He set Pet on the floor and ruffled her hair. "Am I right?"

"Hey, I learned a new trick!" She tugged his arm. "Wanna see me do a cannonball?"

He groaned. "I rest my case."

Rani raised a hand. "I showed her how to put the sofa cushions on the floor and made her swear not to do her tricks without them."

Gage nodded, impressed. "Well, that's progress. Let me write your check, and you can be on your way. I'm sure you have plenty to catch up on after four days cooped up with Pet."

"Anytime. I like her. She's a hoot." Rani faced Zoey. "I made a pot of vegetable soup and some grilled cheese sandwiches for dinner. The sandwiches are on warm in the oven."

"Great. Thanks. I thought I knew the meaning of hungry before, but this pregnancy stuff has taught me a new definition of starved."

Rani glanced at Gage as if she weren't sure she'd heard Zoey correctly. He flashed his babysitter a confident smile and nodded as he tore her check out of his checkbook. "Zoey is due in April. You don't have a problem with keeping a newborn, do you?"

"Uh...no. I..." More confused and startled blinking. "Wow. Congratulations." She accepted the check and stuffed it in her jeans pocket without looking at it. "I'll get out of your hair. You know how to reach me if you need me again."

"You bet." After Gage showed Rani out, he joined Zoey in the living room where Pet was bouncing on the sofa springs and launching herself onto a pile of cushions with an enthusiasm he was sure would translate into more daring escapades before long. God help him. "I can show you to your room now if you want."

Zoey shook her head. "I wasn't kidding about being starved. The room will wait. I'm not sure the baby will. Can we eat first?"

"Whatever. This is your home now. Make yourself comfortable." To Pet, he said, "Okay, Squirt, time to eat. Wash your hands."

Pet ignored him, climbing on the sofa to launch herself onto the cushions again.

Grasping Pet's upper arm, he stopped her as she mounted the sofa the next time and looked straight into her eyes. "Petunia, it's dinnertime. Go wash your hands and sit at the table."

"No! I'm not hungry." Pet tried to pull free, and when he didn't release her, she jumped up and down in place with a haughty smirk on her face.

Gage took a deep breath and knelt in front of his niece, using both hands to hold her as still as a five-year-old monster could be held. "Pet, do you want time-out?"

"No!"

"Go wash your hands."

"No!" she shrieked louder.

He glanced at Zoey, who made a you-weren't-kidding face. "Brace yourself. This is when it gets loud."

Scooping Pet under her arms, he lifted the squirming girl and carried her toward the far corner of the room where a small plastic chair waited. Clearly realizing his destination, Pet loosed a high-pitched scream. As soon as her bottom hit the chair, she wrenched free and flung herself on the ground, kicking at Gage and thrashing like a rabid dog.

Gage pinched the bridge of his nose. Where were the professionals from *Nanny 911* when you needed them? The guys at the fire station would have a field day with him if they knew he'd actually started watching the reality show in hope of picking up some pointers.

But Pet's tantrums frustrated him to the point he felt his temper rise, and he was terrified of one day lashing out with the kind of abuse his father had doled out. He'd rather eat broken glass than hurt Pet, but most days he was at a loss as to how to deal with Pet's bad behavior.

He turned to Zoey, prepared to give her his best I-told-you-so eye roll, when to his amazement, Zoey started screaming at the top of her lungs, as well. She dropped onto the floor and flailed in a tantrum that rivaled anything Pet had mustered. It took only seconds before Pet halted her meltdown to gape at the crazy woman on the floor beside her.

"Um, Zee? What are you doing?" He had to shout to be heard over Zoey's high-pitched, ear-busting screech.

"I'm hungry, and I want to eat! But *she* won't wash her hands!" She pointed at Pet and frowned. "I want to eat! I'm hungry!"

Pet's eyes rounded, and she put her hands over her ears. "Stop yelling!"

"But you won't wash your hands like Gage asked you!" Zoey whined loudly, then continued screaming. "I want to eat!"

Gage stepped backed, bemused, and watched

Pet. His niece looked to him for help, and he shrugged. Finally, Pet stood up with an exasperated huff and stomped her foot. "Okay, okay! You can eat. Be quiet!"

Zoey paused and blinked innocently at Pet. "But we can't eat until you wash your hands."

Pet scowled, clearly sensing she'd been beaten at her own game. When Zoey screamed again, his niece scurried down the hall to the bathroom, where he heard the water come on.

Zoey chuckled under her breath and held her hand out for help getting up from the floor. "Wow. It actually worked."

He hauled her to her feet and met her smug gaze. "Unconventional, wouldn't you say?"

"Maybe. I'm out of my league here. Hate to tell you this, but I haven't a clue how to help you with her. I just thought if she could see how annoying and ridiculous her behavior was that maybe we'd get to the table a little faster."

Pet stomped back through the living room and into the kitchen. Zoey followed his niece and was discussing what had transpired with Pet when he arrived.

"So do you think screaming is a nice way to get what you want or a bad way? Should I do it again?" Zoey asked.

"It's loud and 'noying." Pet gave Zoey a stern look, as if she were the parent. "Don't do that again!"

"I won't if you won't." Zoey placed a steaming bowl of vegetable soup in front of Pet, who took one look at her dinner and wrinkled her nose. Uh-oh.

"This has green stuff in it. I hate green stuff."

Zoey lifted a shoulder. "So don't eat it. More for me. I eat green stuff, even when I don't like it, because I want to grow and be healthy." She blew on a spoonful of soup before she ate it, then tossed a casual glance to Pet. "But I guess you like being shorter than adults and too sick to play outside."

Pet shifted in her chair uneasily. Before long, with a brief explanation of why vegetables were important for a growing girl's health, Zoey had Pet eating her soup and a whole sandwich, even if several of the "green things" were left at the bottom of her bowl.

After Pet carried her dish to the sink—talk about new tricks!—and scampered off to play in the next room, Gage shook his head and squeezed Zoey's hand. "You're a miracle worker. You've accomplished more in an hour than I have in a month of dealing with her."

She scoffed. "Don't be fooled. I'm winging it here. The magic charm of the new aunt will wear off soon enough, and she'll be battling me, too, I'm sure."

"Just the same..." He took his bowl to the stove to refill it. "You've got good instincts. Your methods are...*unusual,* but...I wouldn't expect any less from you."

She snorted a laugh, the mirth in her green eyes making his pulse trip. "Gee, thanks."

His hand tightened on the ceramic bowl, and he quashed the spike of desire with a deep breath. *Just friends.* "You're going to be a great mother, Zee."

Her expression sobered. "Then why am I so scared?"

Chapter 5

After dinner, while Gage read Pet a bedtime story, Zoey used Gage's cell phone to conference call her two sisters. She'd been sitting on the news of her pregnancy, her marriage and her move back to Lagniappe longer than she'd ever kept a secret from her sisters before. But if she kept it quiet from Paige and Holly any longer, she thought her head might explode.

"Zoey, what's…going on?" Holly asked once both her sisters were on the line. "You only conference call us when something major has happened. Are you okay?"

"I'm fine, worry wart. But you're right. I have big news." Zoey paused for dramatic effect.

"You're pregnant!" Paige guessed at the same time Holly blurted, "You got married!"

Zoey frowned. "Have you two talked to Mom and Dad?"

"Why? Has something happened to Mom and Dad?" Holly's voice dipped with concern.

"No, I just thought— Never mind." Zoey took a breath. "You're both right. I'm married, *and* I'm pregnant!" Silence answered her. "Hello? Are y'all there?"

"I—I'm just...surprised," Holly fumbled. "Uh, congratulations."

"You don't sound happy."

"I—I am happy for you, if...if this is what you want. I hope you and Derek will be very happy." Holly's tone was still underwhelming, and disappointment plucked at Zoey.

She'd wanted her sisters to be excited for her, to support her, to help her feel better about her decision. Zoey picked at a loose thread on Gage's recliner. "I didn't marry Derek."

"Wait a minute…" Paige gasped. "My caller ID said Gage Powell when you called."

She heard Holly suck in a sharp breath. "Ohmigod. Did you—?"

"You married Gage!" Paige gushed, cutting off Holly.

"I—"

"It's about time. Everyone who knows you has been expecting you to marry Gage for years!"

Paige's comment caught her off guard. "Excuse me?"

"Is the baby Gage's, too?" Now real excitement vibrated in Holly's voice. "Wh-what happened to Derek?"

"He—"

"Forget Derek," Paige interrupted, "I want to hear about Gage!"

"Well, I'll tell you if you let me finish a sentence!" Zoey said, laughing.

"Okay, okay. We'll be quiet. Right, Paige? Spill, Zoey!"

And she did. For the next half hour, she detailed all the crazy twists and turns of the past couple days, filling in details when one of her sisters questioned her. Paige wanted to know if the baby had been planned, if Zoey had made any contingency plans in case Derek decided he wanted to claim his parental rights to the baby. Her no to both questions didn't go over well with her gotta-have-a-plan sister.

Holly, ever the romantic, wanted to know how she'd felt when she'd learned about the baby and asked how Gage had proposed.

"Happy, but scared. And nauseated. I'm having lots of morning sickness."

"That should pass in a few weeks. At least it did for me," said Holly, who was six months pregnant. "Just think, our babies will be born only a few months apart. It's times like this I wish we lived in Louisiana instead of North Carolina. I want to help you baby shop!"

"I can do that!" Paige said. "Oh, Zoey, it's great to have you home again. We have so much catching up to do. I can't wait for you to meet Jake."

"Same here. He sounds great." Zoey chuckled. "I'm still shocked that you two got married so quickly. I'm supposed to be the rash one."

"What can I say?" Paige chirped, "When you meet the man of your dreams, you don't want to waste another minute without him. Besides, I'd already planned one big church wedding, and we know how that ended! Disaster!"

They all groaned in agreement.

"Gage Powell..." Holly chuckled. "Somehow I always knew you two would end up together. You're perfect for each other!"

Paige had said much the same thing earlier. Zoey's smile faded, rattled by her sisters' assessment. She moved the phone from one ear to the other, stalling. "Well, the thing is...we're not really *married* married."

Paige cleared her throat. "Explain."

Zoey sensed her sisters' disappointment as she detailed the arrangement she'd reached with Gage. Her own unease poked her in the ribs, and she shifted uncomfortably on the recliner. At the back of the house, she heard Gage telling Pet good-night. Closing her door.

"Look, I gotta go. I'll call you again soon."

"Promise me we'll meet one day soon for lunch," Paige said.

"Promise."

"Promise *me* you won't close your heart to the possibility that your marriage to Gage could last," Holly added.

"Maybe," Zoey replied, a bittersweet pang lodged in her heart. "But don't get your hopes up. Making sure our *friendship* lasts is more important than anything else. I'd sacrifice this fake marriage in a heartbeat to protect that bond."

The sound of the shower running woke Zoey the next morning. She roused only enough to realize where she was and feel a wave of security and contentment wash over her. Followed by guilt. She'd spent the night in Gage's king-size bed while he slept on the couch. That was wrong on so many levels.

King-size beds were too big to be slept in alone, and Gage shouldn't be the one to give up his room for her. But Pet had a twin bed in her room, and the third bedroom was crowded with Gage's weight-lifting equipment and assorted junk boxes. This was Gage's house, Gage's bed.

He had a right to be in it. She'd argued as much last night, but he'd put her off, telling her they'd discuss it in the morning.

Zoey rolled over, snuggling deeper into the covers and inhaling the crisp scents that lingered in the sheets and reminded her of Gage. From the master-bathroom shower, she heard Gage sing a line from a nineties rock tune, and she grinned. He was a terrible singer. Yet as she drifted between sleep and wakefulness, her mind conjured an image of Gage, with all his new muscles and masculine brawn, lathering himself and rinsing as he sang. Clouds of steam swirling around his naked body, water streaming down his broad chest, moisture making his dark eyelashes cling and spike, the heat making his skin flush...

Zoey's eyes sprang open. Leapin' lizards! What was she doing harboring sexual fantasies about Gage? She gave her head a brisk shake and determinedly searched for a safe, nonerotic topic. The upcoming autumn holidays. Tag football. Fish-shaped cheese crackers.

Finally she eased back to sleep and didn't

wake again for almost another hour. She smelled coffee from the kitchen, and her stomach growled. The baby was ready for breakfast. If she didn't eat soon, she'd be battling nausea again.

Tossing back the blankets, she grabbed her glasses from the nightstand, stopped by the bathroom to answer nature's call, then headed down the hall where she could hear Gage puttering around the kitchen.

"Morning," she croaked.

Gage turned from the refrigerator and closed the door. "Good morning. Sleep okay?"

Bobbing her head in answer, Zoey raked her hair back from her face and shoved her while-her-contacts-soaked tortoiseshell glasses up her nose. With a yawn, she dragged herself over to the coffeepot, desperate for a java jolt to wake her up and kick-start her brain. She inhaled the rich aroma as she poured, and her mouth watered.

"Uh, Zee?" Gage stepped up beside her and put his hand around her wrist as she tried to lift the mug to her lips.

He smelled crisp and clean like deodorant soap, laundry detergent and cinnamon cereal. Like morning. Like home. And ten times sexier than any pheromone-saturated cologne from a department store. Her pulse fluttered, and she hadn't even had her first sip of coffee. Gage had her adrenaline rushing, her blood heating.

Because he smelled good. Because of his warm grasp on her arm. Because the dark stubble on his jaw reminded her he was no longer a teenage kid but a very masculine grown-up who'd developed an uncanny sex appeal in the past several years. The scar on his chin added a rugged quality to his appearance, even though she knew the sad tragedy behind how he'd gotten the blemish. This early in the morning, before her coffee, her defenses were down. The impulse to snuggle up against him for a drowsy hug and kiss zapped her from nowhere.

"Hmm?" She canted toward him, leaning against his wall of muscle and strength.

"I don't think you're supposed to have caffeine when you're pregnant."

She scrunched her nose, forced her brain to wake up. Caffeine. Coffee. Pregnant.

Then...Gage. She was snuggling against *Gage*. With a spike of alertness, she straightened and stepped away from the warm, supportive chest. She lowered the mug to the counter with a thump, and hot coffee sloshed out. "Oh. Right."

"The caffeine isn't good for the baby. I remember that from when Elaine had Pet." He gave a short humorless laugh as he plucked the mug from her grasp and took a sip. "I read up on the dos and don'ts of pregnancy, because I knew Elaine wouldn't and *someone* had to make sure her baby had a fighting chance to be healthy."

"Yeah, I know. I just forgot." Zoey stared at the coffeemaker with a sinking sense of loss. "No coffee for nine months? I'll never make it. I *need* coffee."

"You can have decaf."

She pulled a face. "Decaf? Seriously?"

"Just sayin'." Gage slid a card in front of her and, handing her a pen, pointed to a line at the bottom. "Sign here, please."

"What's this?"

"I'm adding your name to my checking account. I figure having a joint account will make things easier if you're going to do the shopping and run errands."

"But, Gage—"

He jabbed the card again, and she signed.

"I swear, I'm going to repay you for—"

He pressed a finger to her lips. "Forget it. A joint account is just more practical." He flipped his wrist and checked his watch. "I gotta go." He carried the mug of coffee—*her* mug of coffee...*whimper*—to the breakfast room, where he grabbed his jacket off the back of a chair. "Listen, if you go out today, will you stop by DIY Hut and pick up a part for me?"

He pulled a scrap of paper from his pocket, and she noticed for the first time that he was wearing his fire-department-duty uniform—basic navy pants with a lighter blue, short-sleeved button-down dress shirt decorated with various patches and insignias. Nothing elaborate like a marine's dress blues, but *leapin' lizards*, he looked hot.

She became awkwardly aware of how scruffy she must look in her bedraggled terry bathrobe, ratty "Drama Queen" T-shirt and thick-lensed glasses. She'd never worried before how she looked in front of Gage. He had, in fact, seen her looking pretty gnarly in the past. But this morning she had an odd urge to spiff up for him. At least comb her bed-head hair.

He held the paper out to her. "I wrote the part number down for you. Don't let the sales guy talk you into anything else. I want this specific drill bit. No substitutes. I have an old drill, and this is the only style bit that fits it. This weekend, I'm hoping to start the dollhouse I'm making Pet for Christmas, but I need that bit. Okay?"

She reached for the paper, her hand shaking, and snatched the note from him. To hide the tremor, she jammed her trembling hand in her robe pocket. Jeez, he had her rattled this morning.

"Sure. No substitutes. I got it." She feigned interest in the lapel of her robe to avoid staring at him.

"You okay?" She heard the frown in his voice.

Zoey shrugged. "Nothing. I mean, yeah...caffeine withdrawal is making me jumpy."

"After five minutes?"

She glance up, and her gaze collided with his skeptical, puppy-dog eyes. "I was...*really* addicted to coffee."

"Right." His cheek dimpled when he grinned, and her knees buckled. "Good luck with the monster today. Make sure she keeps her booster seat buckled while you're driving. She's been known to get out and try to crawl into the cargo trunk to wave at the cars behind us."

She touched two straight fingers to her temple in salute. "Keep the monster in her booster seat. Aye, aye, Captain."

"See you tomorrow morning." He headed for the door and was halfway out before his parting registered.

"Wait! Tomorrow?"

He nodded. "That's how our shifts work. Twenty-four on, forty-eight off."

Her jaw dropped. "So I'm here tonight…
alone…with the monster?"

An evil-sounding chuckle rumbled from his
chest. "Yeah. Have fun."

"Wait, Gage, I'm not sure I can do this. I'm
not Mom material!"

"You'll be fine."

Zoey goggled at him. "Tell me again why Pet
doesn't go to kindergarten? You said she was
five. Isn't that old enough?"

"Elaine didn't register her. One of many parental oversights that led me to assume temporary custody. But you're right. She should
be in school. I'll talk to Elaine about permission to sign her up when I call her next time."
Gage bounced his truck keys in his hand once.
"Rani's number is programmed into speed dial
if you need help." He stepped outside, calling,
"So is 911!"

"W—but…" She gaped at his retreating back
through the window in the door.

She was in charge of Pet today. All day. All
night.

"So is 911," she mimicked in a falsetto voice. "*So* not funny."

She staggered back into the kitchen, her head spinning. What did she know about parenting? She'd never even babysat before. Holly was the babysitter, the motherly type.

She crossed to the coffeemaker and gazed longingly at the dark brew simmering in the carafe. No caffeine while she was pregnant. She'd forgotten *that.*

Opening the refrigerator with a jerk, she grabbed the milk and poured a tall glass. Milk was good for a baby, right? Calcium and all...

She sighed, shoulders slumping. She needed to do some serious research on pregnancy. Today. Now. Before Pet woke up. Zoey headed to the corner of the living room where Gage's computer was set up and logged on to the internet. She might have the better part of nine months to learn about caring for a newborn, but she was pregnant *now.* She needed a crash course on the dos and don'ts of being an expectant mother ASAP.

And she had about an hour to figure out how

to parent a little girl before a certain energetic five-year-old woke up and started her day. *Gulp.*

"Aunt Zoey, what do hippopotamuses eat?"

Pet's question jerked Zoey out of her musings as they drove to the mall later that morning. "Um, I've never really thought about it." She paused and gave Pet a suspicious frown via the rearview mirror. "Is this a joke?"

"No! I have to know!" The little girl's wide eyes and desperate tone were comically out of proportion to the situation.

"Why?"

"Because Uncle Gage said that's what he's getting me for Christmas. What will I feed it?"

Zoey covered a laugh and flashed to a Christmas dance in high school where she'd tortured Gage by repeatedly singing "I Want a Hippopotamus for Christmas" as they drove home. Every year since, he'd sworn that was what he was getting *her* for Christmas.

"Tell you what, we'll stop by the pet store while we are at the mall and ask. Okay?"

Pet seemed to wilt with relief. "Oh, good."

As she pulled into the parking lot of the large shopping center, Zoey claimed Pet's attention again. "Hold my hand while we walk inside, okay? And stick close to me. I don't want you to get lost."

Pet bobbed her head. "And I don't want *you* to get lost, either."

Zoey grinned. "Right."

First stop for Zoey was the cellular-phone store where she bought a new phone to replace the one Viper broke. The service tech programmed it to her old phone number, loaded it with her favorite *Annie* ring tone and she was good to go in minutes. Or what seemed like minutes to her. Pet complained bitterly that it was taking too long and flopped on the floor to play hippopotamus, growling at other customers.

When they left the store, hand in hand, Zoey dodged a crowd of spectators where a news crew was filming the reigning Miss Louisiana in a fundraiser for literacy. The beauty queen led a group of schoolchildren through a reading exercise while someone dressed as a blue dog passed out crayons.

Pet eyed the commotion but showed no interest in stopping, so Zoey guided her toward DIY Hut. As they passed a bank of coin-operated kiddie rides, Pet's gaze flew to the brightly painted animals. "I want to ride the horse!"

"Maybe later." Zoey resisted Pet's fervent arm-tugging and continued resolutely toward DIY Hut. The mall, Zoey discovered, was filled with kiddie distractions. By the time they reached DIY Hut, Pet had conned Zoey into a gumball, asked to go in the video arcade and decided she preferred an immediate lunch of chicken nuggets at Chicken King over Burger Barn. The chicken nuggets she got, the video arcade she didn't.

"Can we play hide-and-seek?" Pet asked as Zoey dragged her into DIY Hut, at last.

"That sounds like a good game to play when we get home." Zoey dug the scrap of paper with the drill-bit description from her pocket and sized up the daunting aisles of plugs, screws and adapters. "Stay close, Pet. This could take a while." She gripped the girl's hand and marched down the first aisle that looked promising.

After ten minutes of searching in vain for either the bit or a sales clerk to help her, Zoey was growing frustrated, and Pet was getting restless and whiny. Picking up a drill bit seemed like such a simple request to fulfill, and she hated—no, *refused*—to let Gage down after all he'd done for her. Finally she found the correct aisle, and Zoey scanned the racks of drill parts, checking the stock against Gage's note for brand, part number and size. She'd never known there were so many possible parts for a basic drill.

"Aunt Zoey, what's this?"

She glanced down to see the odd piece of metal Pet had found. "I don't know. Put it back and don't play with stuff, please."

Refocusing her attention on the drill-bit stock, a few of the part numbers started matching up. She was getting closer!

"Aunt Zoey—"

"Pet!" she fussed, her gaze still glued to the plethora of drill-bit options. "If you can just be quiet and patient for a couple more minutes, then I'll be done and we can leave. Okay?"

"Okay." Pet's petulant tone signaled only reluctant cooperation.

"4125...4126! Bingo." Zoey dropped Pet's hand to take the drill-bit package off the display peg, when the bit beside it snagged her attention. "4126T? What's the difference?" She plucked both model numbers off their hooks and read the packages. "Maybe I should get both. I don't see the difference. What do you think, Pet?"

The little girl didn't answer.

"Pet?" Zoey glanced behind her to see what had Pet so occupied that she didn't answer.

The spot where Pet had been standing was empty.

"Pet!" Her gut clenching, Zoey spun around and swept an encompassing glance down the aisle.

Gage's niece was gone.

As seconds grew into minutes without finding Pet, Zoey's concern swelled to panic. After a full five minutes of scouring every DIY

Hut aisle yelling Pet's name, Zoey was nearly hysterical.

Dear God, she'd lost Gage's niece! Her first outing as a parental figure and she'd blown it. Of all her screwups, this blew the others out of the water.

After an initial search hadn't yielded Pet, Zoey had reported Pet's disappearance to the store manager, who'd had the employees close the doors to the mall and man the exits. Every green-vested worker in the store was helping look for Pet from the stock room to the manager's office. But clearly the time had come to call the police.

To call Gage.

The store manager handled the 911 call, while with trembling fingers, Zoey dialed Gage.

He answered with "Hey, I see by my caller ID that you got your new phone."

His statement was so incongruous to the meltdown she was suffering that it took her a few second to reconcile what he'd said. "Uh, yeah…I…Gage—" Her voice cracked, and hot tears leaked onto her cheeks. Guilt sliced a deep swath through her heart. She hated to let him down, to tell him the truth, to show him what a dismal failure and screwup she was.

"Are you crying, Zee?" His tone dipped with compassion. "What's wrong?"

She took a deep breath for courage. "I l-lost Pet."

"*What?*" The word vibrated with disbelief. Shock. Disappointment.

Nausea churned through Zoey, a tidal wave of self-reproach. "I'm so sorry," she rasped, "I only looked away for a minute. I was getting your drill bit, and...and she just...disappeared! We've searched the whole store a dozen times. When I reported her missing, the manager had them lock down the store, but...she must have gotten out the door before—"

"How long has it been?" he interrupted, his tone brisk. "Have you called the cops? Looked in any other stores?"

"It's been about..." she consulted her watch "...twenty minutes now, and the DIY Hut m-manager is calling the police now. H-he notified mall security a couple minutes ago. They've posted guards to watch all the mall exits. I'm headed out into the m-mall now."

"Have they checked the security tape to see if anyone took her?"

She'd been trying hard not to think of that possibility, the idea too horrible to contemplate. Surely she'd have sensed someone, heard someone else in the aisle with them. "Last I heard, Mr. Wilkes, the manager, was having someone check the video."

"Surely the security video will show what happened to her, where she went."

Zoey closed her fist around her purse strap, her palm sweating. "Lord, I hope so, but…h-he said the cameras only scan the store by zone. There can be as long as five-minute gaps in the footage of a specific area." She took another breath, trying to calm herself and think clearly. "Meanwhile I…I have a few more ideas where we can look. We talked about going to the pet store and the horse ride, and she wanted to go in the video arcade, and…" Another sob welled in her throat, choking her. "I wouldn't take her."

Zoey picked up her pace as she jogged toward

the DIY Hut exit into the mall, fresh purpose and hope bubbling to life in her. Ohpleaseohplease!

"Gage, I'm so sorry. I—"

"Meet me at DIY Hut in ten minutes. I'm on my way." With that, he broke the connection.

A chill snaked through her. His curt tone could have been worry, haste or distraction. But she feared it was anger. The kind of exasperated fury that meant he'd finally gotten fed up with her clueless bumbling through life, her wing-and-a-prayer spontaneity, her restless searching for herself at the expense of those around her. She knew *she* was thoroughly sick of her life, but in true Zoey-esque fashion, she had no idea how to change, how to find what she was looking for.

Which made marrying Gage as a stopgap in her current crisis all the more unforgivable. Wiping the tears that blurred her vision, Zoey hurried toward the kiddie rides. No Pet. Next she headed to the pet store. No luck.

She was heading across the mall to the video arcade when she spied the news crew, just packing up from their shoot of the literacy event with Miss Louisiana. Inspiration struck.

If someone had taken Pet, the sooner they got word to the public to watch for the little girl, the better. The more people they had looking for the lost child, the sooner they'd find Pet.

Hitching her purse higher on her shoulder, Zoey sprinted across the food court and stopped the reporter in her tracks. "Excuse me, please. I need your help."

Gage drove like a madman to the Lagniappe Mall, and after leaving his truck, he raced through the parking lot to the door of DIY Hut. Zoey wasn't where he'd asked her to meet him. Seeing a crowd of people gathered a few stores down, he jogged down the mall corridor to see what was happening. The bright lights of a television camera were focused on Zoey, who, with red eyes and tear-stained cheeks was addressing a reporter.

Had something happened? Had they found proof Pet was kidnapped? Was Pet hurt? A thousand terrifying scenarios pummeled him more painfully than his father's fist ever had. Gage shoved his way to the front of the gathered crowd so he could hear.

"...begging anyone with information about Pet's whereabouts to *please* call the Lagniappe police. She's five years old, and has brown eyes and brown hair," Zee pleaded to the camera.

The brunette reporter put the microphone to her own mouth asking, "The girl was in your care when she went missing. Do you feel responsible for her disappearance?"

Gage gritted his teeth. Of all the insensitive...!

"Yes. Absolutely. It was entirely my fault for not watching her closely enough. She's my husband's niece, my niece now, too. I would do anything, *anything* to have a do-over. But since that's not possible, I would do anything to bring her home safely. My family means everything in the world to me, and I would never want them hurt." Her gaze connected with his then, and she bit her bottom lip. She raised her hand in front of the camera lens and faced the reporter. "That's all I have to say. Thank you."

Zoey ducked the giant spotlight next to the cameraman while the reporter said, "That was Zoey Bancroft Powell with an emotional plea for the safe return of her niece, Pet, who went missing just minutes ago at Lagniappe Mall. Anyone with information about the missing girl can call—"

Gage ignored the rest of what the reporter was saying as he dragged Zoey into his embrace. He smoothed her hair, stroked her back, and she clutched his shirt.

"I'msosorry. I'msosososorry," she sobbed into his shoulder.

Guiding her to a more private corner of the food court, he held her at arm's length and gave her the most patient look he could muster. "Zoey, talk to me. Tell me what happened. Tell me where you've looked. Have you seen the security tapes yet?"

She shook her head and swiped her runny nose with her sleeve. "When I saw the news crew, I thought getting the word out, alerting the public would help bring her back faster. More eyes looking for her and all that."

He shrugged, uncertain what value the news crew's broadcast might have. Pet hadn't even been gone an hour, and the mall hadn't been thoroughly searched yet from what he could tell. He dried tears from her cheeks with his thumbs. "Look, Pet disappeared at the grocery store a few weeks ago, too. I was unloading our cart at the checkout, and she slipped away when my back was turned. It took us twenty minutes to find her back in the employee break room under a table with a box of donuts. I should have warned you she's a little Houdini. Before we panic, let's go back to DIY Hut and have a look at the security tapes. Okay?"

Zoey blinked. "You lost her, too?"

"What can I say? The child needs a leash...for her own good. Apparently the scolding I gave her didn't get through to her." He hitched his head toward the main corridor. "Come on. Let's go find the little monster."

When they reached the DIY Hut manager's office, an employee had already scrolled through the footage of the past hour to the time frame closest to when Pet went missing. He clicked on the image for the back of the store and zoomed in on aisle ten. Zoey watched the on-screen version of herself lead Pet into the aisle, pause in front of a rack of drill bits and drop Pet's hand to pluck a package from the display. As on-screen Zoey squinted at the package, her nose wrinkling in confusion, Pet swung her gaze toward the end of the aisle, hunched her back and lifted her hands in an exaggerated tiptoe pose as she sneaked away, glancing back once and covering a giggle as she crept out of the camera shot.

"So she wasn't snatched," the manager said, his tone rife with relief.

"Maybe not then, but what about later?" Zoey moaned. "A little girl alone—"

"It looks to me like she just wandered off on her own," the manager countered.

Gage reached past the employee manning the computer and rewound the video to watch it again. "She's playing hide-and-seek. That's her hide-and-seek sneaky walk."

Zoey gasped, a sinking sensation in her chest.

"She asked if we could play hide-and-seek earlier. I told her we could later, at home."

"So it's just a matter of finding where she's hidden, right?" the kid at the computer controls asked.

"Yeah." Gage blew out a breath from puffed cheeks. "Except she's an extraordinarily good hider. She's small enough to squeeze into some tight spaces and smart enough to find really out-of-the-way places."

"Can we make use of the store's intercom to make an announcement telling her the game is over and to come out?" Zoey suggested.

The store manager was nodding his agreement.

"Can't hurt." Gage stroked a hand down his jaw. "But she's patient and stubborn. She's always stayed hidden until I find her, even if I call for her to come out. One time it took me an hour and ten minutes to find her in a little nook behind my water heater."

Zoey squared her shoulders and tugged Gage's arm. "Well, let's get started. We're not going to find her standing around here."

As she headed to the door of the manager's office, the image playing on the security monitor caught her attention. Heart clutching, she pulled up short and locked her gaze on the screen, hoping her eyes had been playing tricks on her.

The store manager and Gage were in conversation as they filed out of the room, discussing the best use of manpower to find the lost girl.

The kid at the computer pushed out of his chair, but Zoey caught his arm. "Wait." She glanced out of the office, her pulse thumping in her ears, waiting for Gage to be out of hearing. She had to be sure of her suspicion before she raised any red flags.

"C-can you rewind that image for me?" Her hand shook as she tapped the screen indicating a different camera shot than they'd been watching.

The kid shrugged. "Sure. Did you see something suspicious?"

More like someone suspicious.

She held her breath as shoppers milled about

on the screen. Squeezing her fingers around her purse strap, she waited for...

Derek.

Acid flooded her stomach as the lanky figure with the familiar shuffling walk strolled across the screen. She recognized the Arizona Diamondbacks baseball cap that shielded the guy's face from view. Derek had a cap just like it. She'd bought it for him last year on his birthday.

Zoey clutched the back of the chair the computer kid sat in and forced herself to take a calming breath. Derek had several baseball caps. The Diamondbacks cap wasn't even his favorite. And he wasn't the only guy in the country to own the Arizona team's gear. Even though it was rare to see someone in Louisiana sporting the logo of a team from Arizona, it could happen. Right?

You haven't heard the last of me, Red!

Had Derek followed her back to Louisiana? Tailed her this morning? Kidnapped Pet in some sick game of revenge or blackmail? Black spots swam in her vision, and blinking hard to clear her sight, she locked her knees when her legs threatened to buckle.

"See what you were looking for?" the kid asked, glancing over his shoulder.

Zoey swallowed hard, wetting her suddenly arid throat so she could respond. "I—I've seen enough. Th-thank you."

Don't panic. Just because the guy on the security tape looked like Derek didn't mean it was him. She hadn't seen his face. The guy didn't have a little girl with him. And Derek, for all his other unsavory characteristics, wasn't low enough to kidnap a child. At least the Derek she'd believed herself in love with wouldn't, but…she hadn't thought he'd rob her blind and reject his own baby, either. A nausea that had nothing to do with her pregnancy swamped her.

What was she supposed to do?

Gage stuck his head back in the office doorway. "Comin', Zee?"

She sucked in a reinforcing breath and nodded briskly. "Yeah, uh…r-right behind you."

Gage took her hand and tugged her toward the

front entrance of the store. "DIY Hut employees are going to search the store again. You and I should start looking in the other shops, spreading the word to the rest of the store managers."

She followed in his wake, battling mentally over whether to tell him what she'd thought she'd seen on the security tape. *Who* she'd seen. Except she wasn't sure.

If she accused Derek and was wrong, they could waste precious time chasing a false lead. But if she was right...

"Gage, wait. After you left the office, I...I saw something on the security tape you should know about."

Turning to her, he cocked his head, giving her his attention. "Did you see where she hid?"

"No, but I thought I saw...Derek."

Gage's spine drew poker straight. "Define 'thought you saw.'"

She explained how the Diamondbacks cap on the man in the tape was like one she knew her ex owned, how similar his walk was.

"But Pet wasn't with him? And you didn't see his face?"

"Right. I know it's not much to go on, but…"

"No, it's not." Gage stepped closer, inside her personal space. She could smell the fresh soap scent still on him from that morning. He skimmed his fingers along her jaw and settled his hand on the nape of her neck. "Look, don't panic. We *know* Pet crept away from you using her 'sneaky walk.' On her own.

"We'll let mall security know about this guy, but they already have all the exits monitored. Let's finish searching the mall before we borrow trouble. I honestly think she's just playing hide-and-seek, and we just have to find her." His thumb strummed down the bumps made by the vertebrae in her neck, and a sense of calm washed through her. He'd always helped keep her centered, reeled her in when she tended to fly off on an emotional tangent.

But as they jogged out to the main corridor of the mall and headed toward the next shop, one overwhelming fact loomed over her like a black cloud. She'd been responsible for Pet and had let the girl slip away. Whether her ex had a hand in this was uncertain, but she knew deep in her heart that Pet's disappearance was entirely her fault.

For the next two hours, Gage and Zoey helped the mall security and the employees of the numerous stores search high and low for Pet. An infinite number of clothing display racks, closets, kiosks and shelves were searched and searched again. The troubled gnawing in Gage's stomach bit harder the more time passed. His confidence that finding Pet was just a matter of time, his certainty that his niece was somewhere in the mall hiding dimmed as the minutes ticked away. A real and wrenching fear that Pet could have been kidnapped or wandered away from the mall took root and shook him to the core. *I thought I saw Derek.*

Gage shook off the foreboding that slithered through him. What would Derek have to gain from snatching Pet?

Zoey's scumbag ex hadn't been happy about her leaving Vegas, but Derek's gripes had seemed self-centered, not about losing Zoey per se. His issue had been with her cutting off his source of cash. But if he'd taken Pet to demand a ransom, wouldn't they have heard from Derek by now?

Gage clenched his back teeth and shoved down the swell of acid in his gut. He needed to stay in control, not let Zoey see his worry or she'd freak.

Zoey climbed to her feet after checking under a display table in the linens store on the farthest end of the mall. He offered her a hand, helping her to her feet.

"This is all my fault," she groaned. "I'm a walking disaster. A total screwup. You of all people should know that. I can't imagine why you hang around, why you stick by me."

"First of all, it's not your fault. If either of us is to blame, I am, for not disciplining Pet properly last time this happened to teach her how dangerous this kind of stunt is."

Zoey shook her head, and he caught her cheeks between his hands.

"For the record, I have plenty of reasons to

stick by you. Besides the fact that you're my wife now, you're my best friend."

"But I'm a disas—"

"You're *not* a disaster. You're a…a free spirit. Spontaneous."

Her face fell. "I wish I were more like Paige… or Holly. They're—"

"I don't. As much as I like your sisters, they're not you. I love that you're different."

"I don't see how you can say that after today."

"Everyone makes mistakes sometimes."

"You're too forgiving." Her guileless but dubious eyes stared back at him. Gage battled down the impulse to kiss away her fears, steeling himself as he had all through high school against her magnetic gaze.

If he wanted to help Zoey, he first had to protect his own heart. He had to be strong enough for both of them.

"I'm just being practical."

She lifted an auburn eyebrow and opened her mouth to reply, probably to deny his assertions, but the refrain of "Tomorrow" from the musical *Annie* blasted from her cell phone. The notes jangled down his spine with an eerie déjà vu. For years after she starred in the musical at school, she'd annoyingly sung the chipper tune to him whenever he got down.

She fumbled in her purse and flipped open her phone. "Hello? Yes?"

He held his breath and studied her face, eager to know if the call was good news...or bad.

"She was wearing a pink shirt and red pants with daisies." Zoey chewed her lip. Her anxious expression didn't bode well, and Gage's heart-beat slowed.

Please let Pet be all right.

Chapter 6

Interminable seconds ticked by as he waited for some signal from Zoey what was happening. Had they found Pet? Was his niece hurt?

He signaled to her and raised his palms in question. "What? Tell me."

She waved him off, hushing him. "Where? Really?" Her face brightened. "Oh, thank God!" Lifting a glowing smile to him, she clapped a hand to her chest, laughing and crying at the same time. "We'll be right there!"

The smothering knot in Gage's chest loosened. "Someone found her?"

Her eyes wet and her smile beaming, Zee bounced on her toes and grabbed his arm. "At Chic Boutique. She'd fallen asleep in the janitor's closet behind an old floor-display sign."

He scrubbed both hands over his face, and the tension inside him melted, leaving an over-supply of adrenaline quaking in his muscles. "Thank God. Let's go take our girl home."

That afternoon, once they'd assured the swarm of media that had descended on their doorstep that all was well and no further interviews would be granted, Gage and Zoey sat Pet down for a firm lecture.

"Uncle Gage?" Pet said when Gage finished explaining why what she'd done was dangerous and bad behavior. "Aunt Zoey told a man at the store she wanted to kiss him." She covered a simpering grin with her hand and giggled.

Gage shot Zee an inquiring look, and she rolled her eyes.

"He helped me find the drill-bit aisle when I was lost, so I said, 'I could kiss you.' It's just an expression!"

He knew the incident meant nothing, but he couldn't help lowering his gaze to her lips.

"Zoey and store man sittin' in a tree. K-i-s-s-i-n-g!" Pet bounced on the couch as she sang.

When he continued to stare at her, Zoey grunted and puckered her mouth in a moue of discontent that only drew more attention to her raspberry-tinted lips. He'd been battling the urge to kiss her ever since she first fell into his arms, sobbing with fear for Pet at the mall.

Ever since their kiss at the Las Vegas wedding chapel.

Hell, ever since her perfectly bowed lips had sent him a lopsided smile of friendship in junior high.

Zoey drilled him with a what-are-you-doing stare and aimed a finger at Pet, who still chanted her taunting rhyme.

"That's enough, Pet. I told you the last time you hid from me in a store that there'd be consequences if you did it again."

Pet scratched her nose. "What's conwences?"

"It means you're in trouble. What you did

today was bad behavior, and I have to punish you."

Pet's eyes welled with tears. "No! I promise I'll be good!"

His niece's trembling chin broke his heart, and he almost balked. "No TV for a week."

Pet shrieked her dismay and bolted from the room. "I hate you!" she screamed before she slammed her bedroom door.

He faced Zoey, hoping for sympathy and support. Instead, she glared at him.

"Great. And *what* am I supposed to do to keep her out of trouble all week if she can't watch TV?" Her eyes flashing, Zoey shoved to her feet and stomped into the kitchen.

Gage sighed. *Sheesh.* Life with two volatile females—an out-of-control five-year-old and a hormonal pregnant woman. Heaven help him.

In the kitchen, Zoey yanked open the refrigerator and stared into it. She needed a snack. Her pregnancy had turned her into an eating machine. While she hadn't had any of the infamous cravings yet, she definitely had discovered some odd aversions. The smell of brown sugar, usually a favorite of hers, now turned her stomach. The same with oregano. Italian food held no appeal to her anymore.

She pulled out the bucket of leftover fried chicken they'd picked up on the way home from the mall and bit into a cold drumstick.

What was she supposed to do with Pet this week during her TV ban? The idea of taking Pet to the park to play left her in a cold sweat. Too many opportunities for the monster to break a bone or get lost again. Arts and crafts? Messy, but doable. She prayed Pet wouldn't eat the glitter or glue her fingers together or something. And when was she supposed to find a job to pay Gage back if she was on Pet duty all day, every day? Sinking onto a kitchen chair, she raked her hair back from her face, then scoffed, realizing she had chicken grease on her fingers. And now in her hair. *Grrr.*

As she ate, her mind drifted back to those bone-chilling hours of dread and worry before they'd found Pet. She remembered looking past the bright camera lights as the news crew broadcast her plea for help and seeing Gage in the crowd of spectators. She'd been on the verge of flying apart, coming completely undone when he'd pulled her into his arms and made everything right. Even if just for a few seconds. His presence at her side as they'd searched the mall had kept her sane. He'd remained cool under pressure when she'd wanted to tear her hair out. But then, his job as a fireman required that he respond to a crisis with levelheaded thinking and calm logic.

And years of dealing with the turbulence of his abusive father, erratic sister and alcoholic mother had trained him well for crisis management.

Her cell phone sang to her from her purse, and abandoning the drumstick, she dragged herself to the counter to retrieve her cell. She poked the answer button with the tip of her greasy finger and hastily wiped her hand on a kitchen towel. "Hello?"

"So I saw you on the news tonight, crying about Gage's kid being lost."

Hearing the familiar male voice, she stiffened.

"I take it you found her in the closet where I left her," Derek said.

"Where *you left her?*" The food in her stomach soured. "Then you *did* take her, you scum! I thought I saw you on the security tape!"

"Hey, back up. I didn't take her!" Derek sounded truly offended. "The kid wanted to play hide-and-seek. I just helped her hide from you." He chuckled, low and taunting. "Scared ya, huh?"

Zoey gritted her teeth. "What do you want, Derek?"

"You know what I want. Money." She heard muffled voices in the background before he continued. "We got us a problem with Viper. He wants his cash, and he's getting real testy."

Zoey fisted her hand and dug her fingernails into her palms. "News flash, Derek. Viper and his buddies are your problem, not mine."

"Actually..." Derek's tone held a disturbing note of unease. "Viper knows you got money, and he says he'll let me off the hook if you'll cover what I owe him."

"Then you're out of luck. Because you stole all of my money and gambled it away. Remember?"

"Yeah, but you're back in with your family and your pal Gage. So..."

A chill crawled through her. "So?"

Derek cleared his throat nervously. She heard desperation creep into his voice. "So, surely they have money. Mom and Dad are rich. Hubby's bound to have something stashed away that he'd share with his new wife."

Her laugh held no humor. "*No.* No way in hell. I'm through letting you bilk me for everything I have. Take a hike, Derek." She hung up, regretting that she had only a tiny button to push instead of a handset she could slam onto the phone base. As she stood in the middle of Gage's kitchen, trembling with fury, her phone rang again.

She ignored it, letting Annie belt out the full refrain of "Tomorrow" before the call kicked over to voice mail.

Zoey closed her eyes and sighed. She didn't need Derek harassing her today of all days. She'd thought she'd put him behind her when she married Gage and moved back to Lagniappe. Clearly she'd been wrong.

Her phone buzzed, alerting her to a new text. Derek, no doubt. Knowing she should delete the text unread, she thumbed her keypad until the message appeared.

I'd hate for anything to happen to Pet.

Bile climbed Zoey's throat. Had Pet's disappearance at the mall today been part of a scheme to get money from her? While she didn't think Derek would ever hurt a child—she'd lived with him long enough to know he wasn't violent—she couldn't rule out the risk Viper posed.

When her phone rang again, she answered the call, her voice cracking. "H-hello?"

"Please, Zoey, you gotta help me out. Tell you what, you come up with a thousand bucks, and I won't tell Viper and his friends where you've moved or how to find your family. Deal?"

When her knees buckled, Zoey stumbled to a chair before her legs gave out. Icy fear slithered through her veins. "You cretin. Why are you doing this to me? Leave me alone!"

"What'd you say?" Gage called from the living room.

Her heart kicked. She hadn't realized how loud she'd been. "Uh…nothing. Just talking to myself." Turning away from the door to the living room, Zoey pitched her voice low. "Don't you dare try to threaten me, Derek."

"I don't want to drag your family into this, but I've got no one else to ask. You can get that money. I know you can. You owe me."

Her jaw dropped. "I owe you nothing!"

"You told that reporter that you'd do anything to get that kid back. That your family, quote, *means everything in the world to me, and I would never want them hurt,*" he said, panic filling his voice. "Viper will come after you, too, if we don't give him what he wants!"

The chicken in Zoey's stomach sat like a rock as her apprehension grew.

"If your family really means that much to you, you'd want to protect them from Viper. I'd hate for that little girl to go missing for real."

She gasped. "You wouldn't!"

"Or for your parents to have an unfortunate accident."

"Derek, no!"

"Or for that new husband of yours to—"

"All right!" she blurted, just wanting the terrifying threats to stop. The hard edge in his voice told her how desperate he'd become. Fear for his own life had turned him into this coldhearted beast. Tears welled in her eyes, and she sighed her resignation. "I'll do it."

What choice did she have? She had to protect her family. Derek had already shown how easily he could destroy the delicate balance in her life.

She'd already caused Gage and her parents so much grief with her screwups in recent years. She'd sworn not to hurt them anymore. If giving Derek a little money would make him go away then...she'd find a way to wire him the cash.

"Then we have a deal? You'll send me the grand?"

She chafed at the relief in Derek's voice. "Only if you promise...no, *swear* to me that you'll leave my family alone. Keep Viper away from them."

"I'll try, but..."

"Do more than try, Derek. You can't—"

"I need the money first thing tomorrow," he interrupted. He gave her the address of a motel outside of town where she was to wire the cash.

Anger and disgust writhed in her chest. But was it for Derek or herself?

"Okay. But promise me that—" She heard a click that told her he'd hung up on her.

With a heavy heart and trembling hand, she keyed off her phone and stared blankly at the crayon drawings Pet had taped to the refrigerator.

Gage called Pet a monster, but the real beast, the real evil presence in her life had tracked her down just when she was making a fresh start, trying to turn her life around.

Desperation and fear had made Derek a dangerous adversary. To protect the people she loved from that danger, she'd made a deal with the devil.

* * *

Later that night, after Pet had finally fallen asleep, Zoey sat on the edge of Gage's bed, rubbing lotion into her feet, when Gage came in and sat down beside her.

"What a day, huh?" He pinched the bridge of his nose.

"I'll say." *And you don't even know about Derek's call.*

"So now you've seen why I need help with Pet. She's killing me." He barked a dark, sarcastic laugh. "No wonder Elaine drinks."

Zoey slanted a scowl at him. "Not funny."

"I know," he sighed.

Should she tell Gage about Derek's threats, his extorting money from her? She chewed her bottom lip, waffling. Why should she burden Gage with any more of her problems? With any luck, Derek would take the money she'd send him tomorrow and finally disappear from her life. She prayed that giving Derek what he wanted now would finally put an end to her problems with him, and Gage never had to find out. Once she had a job, she'd add the money to their joint account, and Gage would never know. She hoped.

In the meantime, she had more immediate problems to deal with. Namely, Pet and her own impending motherhood. She brushed a stray wisp of her hair away from her eyes with the back of her hand and groaned. "I'm not ready to be a mother. I mean, crap! I lost your niece the very first day I took care of her."

"Again…not your fault."

She pulled a face, telling him she didn't buy it.

"Well, not entirely your fault. All's well that ends well."

"Yeah, but what if it hadn't ended well?"

Picking up the bottle of lotion, Gage squirted a generous amount into his palm and lifted her foot to his lap. Silently he began working the lotion into her tired feet.

After hours of walking the mall, first shopping, then looking for Pet, Zoey's dogs were barkin'. Gage's strong fingers massaged her arch with deep, relaxing rubs that made her bones melt. She moaned and flopped back onto the mattress. "Aw, man, you have magic hands."

He wiggled his eyebrows. "You like?"

"Uh-huh."

"Just imagine what these hands could do..." he gave her a sultry look that fired a heat in her belly "...*other* places."

She didn't have to imagine. She'd learned firsthand on graduation night how talented Gage's hands were. And his lips. And his—

A shudder raced through her, and she snatched her feet from his lap. Heart pounding, she lurched off the bed and tugged the belt of her terry robe tighter.

"Zee?"

Facing him, she propped a hand on her hip. "You promised. It was one of the rules I made. Remember? No sex. Last time we slept together, it..." She waved a hand searching for the right words.

"Last time was incredible. Unforgettable. Admit it." He kept his voice pitched low, and the baritone notes slid over her skin like a caress.

He was right, of course. But that was the

problem. Sex with Gage had been so good it scared her. Heaven knows, sex since that first time with Gage hadn't been nearly as earth-shaking or powerful.

But she wasn't supposed to have slept with her best friend. Maybe she'd just thought it was good because she'd been drinking. Or maybe she'd just wanted it to be good because it was her first time. Losing your virginity was supposed to be…awkward and painful and embarrassing, so when it wasn't, she'd been all the more confused. And while losing your virginity was supposed to be momentous and emotional, she hadn't been prepared for the surge of deeply tender and tangled feelings for Gage that had bombarded her the next morning.

If she was being honest, that night had been pity sex. Gage had been devastated by his family's disinterest in his graduation, and having confronted his drunk father, he'd returned blows for the first time with his abusive old man, defended himself. For his efforts, Gage had earned a black eye and a load of guilt and heartache. Zoey's attempts to comfort Gage, who'd shed rare tears in the Bancrofts' pool house, had rapidly gotten out of hand and turned sexual while their respective defenses and inhibitions were down.

Staring at him now, Zoey crossed her arms over her chest and fought off the poignant memories. "Last time was a mistake."

When his shoulders drooped and he looked away, she tensed. "It was, Gage! We could have ruined our friendship. It almost *did* ruin it. Everything got so complicated and weird, I freaked out and left town. Things were awkward between us for years afterward. We grew apart. I...I don't want that to happen again. You mean too much to me. I need your friendship a hell of a lot more than I need sex."

And she didn't want to create any new bonds between them that, when broken, would cause more pain when they went their separate ways in a year or so. So much could go wrong between now and then. It wasn't so much a matter of *if* she messed up again as *when*. Today only proved that point.

Gage rose from the bed, nodding slowly.

"Fine. A promise is a promise." He handed her the bottle of lotion and headed for the door. "If you need me, I'll be on the couch."

"About that…"

He hesitated.

"If we build a kind of wall between us with pillows, I don't see why you can't sleep here, in the bed. This king is huge. We can share, don't you think?"

He stepped back in the bedroom. "Up to you. Are you okay with sharing?"

She glanced at the wide bed and nodded confidently. "Sure. No problem."

With a deep breath, she tried to tamp down the squiggly feeling in her gut. *Famous last words…*

The next morning, Zoey wired Derek the money she'd promised, and after two weeks passed with no further threats from him, she began to believe her problems with him had been solved.

When October passed without further contact, she allowed herself to breathe easily again.

Her arrangement with Gage settled into a comfortable routine, and the guilt she felt for imposing herself on Gage's life faded from black to dark gray. Her morning sickness eased. Her baby bump grew. She read copious amounts of information about pregnancy and caring for a newborn, and with permission from Elaine, she enrolled Pet in kindergarten. Elaine, Gage said, had sounded excited about Pet joining school, having some normalcy in her world.

Life was looking up all around.

Being in school did wonders for Pet. She had a positive outlet for her curiosity and energy so that she was calmer when at home. The structure and discipline of the classroom gave her boundaries and a model of behavior she was eager to match to please her teacher. At a parent–teacher conference at the end of Pet's first week of school, the kindergarten teacher gave Gage and Zoey a book with numerous tips on effective discipline and teaching young children how to stay safe. Zoey pored over the book, soaking in the information, not just for help with Pet, but so she'd be prepared to raise her baby, as well.

She found an obstetrician she trusted and started regular prenatal visits. Gage accompanied her to her first doctor appointment, and when the doctor pointed out her baby's fluttering heartbeat on the ultrasound screen, tears filled Zoey's eyes. She clutched Gage's hand and fought for a breath. "Ohmigod, look at my baby!"

Zoey angled her gaze toward Gage. He watched the screen with a guarded expression, his jaw tight and his brow furrowed. He seemed restless, ill at ease. Distant. When he met her eyes, she smiled, hoping to draw him out. He knew she wouldn't force her baby on him after it was born. Their marriage agreement expired after the baby came and she was back on her feet financially.

He returned a crooked smile that didn't reach his eyes. And left her feeling oddly unsettled.

She shoved the incident aside, telling herself she'd read too much into it. Things were going well in her life for a change, and she didn't want to rock the boat by pressing Gage about his intentions toward her baby. She'd been looking for a job she could do while Pet was in school, but with the local economy in the tank and no college degree, she'd found nothing. Gage insisted she didn't need to go to work, that he could provide for them, if not lavishly. But repaying Gage was a matter of pride, so her job search continued.

October faded into November, and on Friday mornings, it became Zoey's weekly custom, while Pet was at school, to meet her oldest sister, Paige, and go baby shopping. They shopped for Zoey's baby, but also for gifts for Holly, whose first baby was due not long after Christmas. When they finished shopping, they would meet their mother for lunch at a trendy tea shop, another new weekly ritual. Zoey savored the chance to spend time with her mother and Paige and rebuild the close ties she'd damaged when she left home with Derek.

Holly, her husband, Matt, and Matt's two children from his first marriage were arriving early next week for Thanksgiving, and a huge family gathering was in the works. Zoey looked forward to sharing the holiday with her parents, her sisters and their new husbands. The Bancroft conclave would also give Holly's new family a chance to get acquainted with Gage and Pet. *Her family.*

Even if only for a few months, Gage and Pet were *her* family, and a sense of pride and belonging bloomed in her chest when she thought of sharing her new family with the rest of the Bancroft clan. For once, she wouldn't have to pretend the shadow of her successful, well-adjusted, purpose-driven sisters didn't hover over her.

Yet even with all the changes in her life, the more positive direction her life was moving, nagging fears lurked at the edges of every family dinner with Pet and Gage, every shopping trip with Paige, every prenatal doctor appointment. All her newfound happiness was a china ball poised at the edge of a precipice. The slightest bump would spell disaster, shattering the fragile life she'd created.

Every time the phone rang, she expected

Derek to be at the other end of the line. Her own penchant for rash decisions and attracting trouble loomed like a thundercloud on the horizon each morning. Any day could be the day she messed up again and brought misery down on the people she loved.

And despite her confident promise to Gage that sharing his big bed would be no problem, she fought a nightly battle with herself not to snuggle up to his broad chest and inviting body heat. Only constant reminders of the valued friendship she stood to lose kept her on her side of the bed, listening to Gage's even breaths as he slept.

The nights he was on duty at the fire station, she'd stare at his empty pillow, missing the easy chatter they shared, discussing the mundane, planning for the coming weekend and laughing at private jokes as they drifted off to sleep. Talking to Gage had always been so easy and so important to her. With him, she was an open book. Almost from the beginning of their friendship, she'd shared everything with Gage and vice versa.

Which meant keeping the money she'd paid Derek a secret from Gage gnawed at Zoey like an ulcer. But she knew he'd never understand that she'd done it to protect all of them.

He couldn't understand what he'd done wrong. Gage leaned back in the kitchen chair at the firehouse and shook his head. He'd checked his math with a calculator three times, double checked his bank statement, but his account balance was still one thousand dollars off.

"What's that frown about, Powell? Newlyweds are supposed to be all smiles."

Gage glanced up at his fellow firefighter, Riley Sinclair, as he strolled in from the rec room and pulled open the refrigerator.

Gage returned the front legs of the ladder-backed chair to the floor and hunched over the paperwork spread in front of him. "I'm trying to balance my checking account, and I can't figure out why I'm so far off."

"I assume you've verified all your math. Usually for me it's just a boneheaded subtraction error." Riley poured himself a glass of milk and joined Gage at the table.

"Yep. Gone over it three times. No outstanding checks unaccounted for and—" He stopped when he noticed a withdrawal listed on the back of the bank statement where the transactions had carried over one extra line. "Hold the phone... What the hell is this?"

Riley finished his milk and swiped his mouth with his sleeve. "Something wrong?"

"They've got a one-thousand-dollar withdrawal on here that I didn't make." He grunted and slapped his hand on the table in frustration. "Guess I'll be wrangling with the bank tomorrow over their poor accounting. What a hassle."

"You sure Zoey didn't make that withdrawal and forget to record it?"

"Well...no." Gage folded his bank statement and shoved it back into his file folder, reminding himself that the joint account had been his idea.

Riley grinned. "Welcome to the Married Men Whose Wives Spend All the Money Club.

Ginny's not *too bad* about spending without consulting me, but…she's still a woman, if you know what I mean. Retail therapy is her favorite way to reduce stress."

Gage sent Riley a sympathetic smile, then glanced at his watch. "It's too late to call and ask her about it now." He rubbed his thumb on the edge of his checkbook folder. "Thousand dollars is a lot. Why would she need that much?"

Riley snorted. "No telling. Say, isn't her family loaded? Maybe she's just got expensive habits and isn't used to having to account for her cash."

A rumble of unease rolled through Gage. "Yeah, her family's real well-off, but—"

"Who's real well-off?" Hunter Mansfield asked as he entered the kitchen and dumped his dirty dishes in the sink.

Riley hitched his head toward Gage. "His wife's family."

Hunter whistled. "You lucky son of a gun. Zoey have any sisters?"

Gage nodded absently, his mind stuck on

Riley's comment about the lifestyle Zoey was accustomed to. "Two. Both married."

Hunter chuckled. "Damn, I'm too late."

"Hate it for ya, pal." Riley slapped Hunter on the back as the rookie firefighter left the room.

Gage tapped his checkbook against his palm, staring at the table without really seeing. Having grown up surrounded by wealth and privilege, Zoey was bound to have financial expectations he couldn't meet on his salary. Somehow asking her to adhere to his sparse budget felt like a failure. He wanted to give her the moon, and knowing he could barely afford the MoonPies that Pet loved, especially while he was paying for Elaine's detox care, chafed his ego.

He may have come a long way since leaving his family's dilapidated trailer, but he was a far cry from living up to the four-car-garage-and-pool-house lifestyle Zoey had known all of her life. Why had he ever thought he could make Zoey happy long-term?

The devil inside him, a voice a lot like his father's, whispered to him. *You're a stopgap, a stepping stone out of a bad situation for her, and the sooner you come to terms with that the better.* When Zoey grew weary of generic-brand groceries and tightening their financial belt until they couldn't breathe, would she flee their marriage of convenience and move on with her life?

Probably.

For as long as he'd known Zoey, she'd been restless, free-spirited, straining against the reins of convention and the confines of their Louisiana town. He'd be wise to remember that something as restrictive as marriage, parenting a wild little girl and living in walking distance of her parents' estate would never be enough for Zoey.

And he'd be wise to keep a tight rein on his feelings for her. If the past eleven years of his loyalty and devotion hadn't made her feelings for him change, why would trapping her in a life of the very conventions she'd rebelled against for years change her heart?

With a deep centering breath, he reminded himself that this faux-marriage was about protecting Zoey. Helping Zoey. Saving her from herself and getting her back on her feet. He needed to keep that priority in sharp focus, keep his emotional walls in place and his libido locked down. Living with Zoey, sleeping next to Zoey, watching Zoey grow a baby inside her was testing his willpower to its limits. But he had years of experience guarding his heart. To save Zoey. To save their friendship, to save himself, he could keep his feelings in check as long as he had to. He had no other choice.

Chapter 7

On the Friday before Thanksgiving, the last day she could shop and have lunch Pet-free until the school's weeklong Thanksgiving vacation was over, Zoey sat in a favorite sandwich shop with Paige and their mother, cooing over the infant-size socks she'd bought that morning, when her cell phone rang. Distracted by her sister's oohs and her mother's aahs, Zoey pressed the phone to her ear without checking the caller ID. "Hello?"

"Viper's looking for another installment on our debt. I need more money, Red."

The familiar voice sent ice sluicing through her veins. Zoey squeezed her phone tighter and fought down the wave of panic clawing her throat. Schooling her expression so as not to draw undue attention from her mother and sister, she rose from their table and walked toward the ladies' restroom. "No," she whispered harshly as she crossed the restaurant. "I told you before to leave me alone. You're not getting any more money from me, Derek, so buzz off!"

"I can't, Zoey. I need your help. I owe Viper more than ever now. I thought I could win some cash, but…I lost. Please, Red. Help me out. I don't know where else to go."

She smacked the door to the bathroom open with the flat of her palm. "I've given you all I can, Derek. So don't call again."

"Don't hang up, Red. Please. I'm askin' as nice as I can. You gotta give me some money. I'm begging."

"When hell freezes."

"Zoey, don't be like that."

She gritted her teeth. *"Goodbye,* Derek."

She'd poised her finger over the end button when he said, "I have something you want."

Zoey hesitated. Something she wanted? Could he have kidnapped Pet from her school? Had he broken into Gage's house and stolen something valuable?

A tickle of suspicion and dread made her raise the phone to her ear again. "You're bluffing. You have nothing."

"Oh, but I do. I have my paternal rights to our kid." His tone changed, as if he'd just discovered he held the golden egg.

Zoey felt her heartbeat still for a moment before her pulse kicked into overdrive. "You said you didn't want this baby, you jerk!"

"That was then. This is now."

Her muscles trembled, and she stumbled into a stall. Sinking onto a toilet before her legs gave out, she propped an elbow on her knee and buried her face in her hand. "Are you threatening me?"

The question she'd intended to sound tough and defiant, warbled from her throat.

Derek sighed and lowered his voice. "Naw,

Zoey, I just…You gotta help me get Viper off my back. He beat the crap outta me last night. Says he'll give me more of the same if I don't give him his money, plus interest, by Monday."

Her gut clenched, imagining Derek, a man she'd once believed she loved, the father of her baby, beaten and bloody. "Derek, I can't—"

"Please, Red. I need your help. I'm in over my head." She recognized the sweet, little-boy tone of his plea.

He was playing on her vulnerabilities. The consummate poker player, he'd learned her tells, discovered her weaknesses and how to exploit them. He knew how much she hated the idea of anyone she cared about getting hurt. Especially because of her. She'd fretted about her feud with her father and talked about her graduation-night fiasco with Gage enough times to give that much away.

He knew she always rooted for the underdog on principle, had a romantic streak a mile wide and a heart made of marshmallow. Because she was so uncertain what she wanted most of the time, she was putty to him, bending to his will with the slightest persuasion. Where his manipulation had been only mildly irritating when they were together, she now saw its devastating potential.

"Do it for our baby. You wouldn't want anything to happen to your baby's father, would you?"

In her heart, she'd begun to think of Gage as the baby's father. Now Derek was threatening to take her child from her.

Bile burned her throat. The walls of the bathroom seemed to close in on her. "Leave the baby out of this."

"Can't do that. The baby is part of this. He ties us together. Links us."

"*No!* You lost any right to the baby when—"

"I changed my mind. Maybe I want visitation rights. Hell, maybe I want custody." An edge of cold menace had returned to his voice. Derek's desperation made him mean, gave him the motivation to hurt her if it got him what he wanted. "How much is it worth to you to avoid a drawn-out custody fight? Court-ordered visitation?"

She blinked back tears of frustration and fear.

"You're a bastard, Derek. You don't care about this baby! Why are you doing this to me?"

"You made me resort to this. If you'd just help me... Zoey, you have access to money I don't."

She heard the restroom door open and close. "Zoey, honey, are you all right? You left the table so fast, and you looked upset."

Zoey stiffened. *Her mother.*

"I have to go," she grated in a whisper and hung up before Derek could respond.

Swiping moisture from her eyes, she stood, blew her nose on some bathroom tissue and flushed the commode. "I'm fine, Mom. I just... um, couldn't hear well in the restaurant, so..."

With a deep breath to gather her composure, Zoey stepped out of the stall and flashed her mother a forced grin.

"Was that Gage?" Ellen's gaze assessed Zoey. "Is something the matter?"

"No, nothing like that. I..." As she shoved her phone in her pocket, she fumbled for an excuse that wasn't a lie. "It was a guy...soliciting a donation." Ducking her head, Zoey feigned an intense interest in washing her hands.

"Oh. Well, Paige and I were discussing the menu for Thanksgiving. When you're finished—"

"I am." She trashed the paper towel she'd dried her hands on and followed her mother back to their table.

Paige was in the middle of describing a dessert she wanted to bring to Thanksgiving dinner when Zoey's phone rang again. Her stomach pitched. Was this how it would be until she gave in to Derek's demands? Constant harassing phone calls and threats?

"Sorry." She gave Paige a sheepish grin and pulled out her phone. The caller ID showed an unfamiliar local number. Concerned that it could be Pet's school, Zoey answered the call.

"So what will it be, Red? Five thousand dollars or a custody battle?"

She felt the blood leak from her face, but she croaked, "I'm afraid you have the wrong number."

This time when she disconnected, she turned off her phone. If there was an emergency with

Pet, the school had Gage's number at the fire station.

Her stomach churning with anger and anxiety, Zoey couldn't eat anything else. She employed her best acting skills to hide her consternation from her mother and Paige. The last thing she wanted as she tried to repair her damaged relationship with her family was for anyone to find out ghosts of her past mistakes still lurked in the shadows, ready to cause more heartache for the people she cared about most.

As much as she hated the idea of giving Derek any more money, she hated the idea of letting her family down more. Even the suggestion that Derek could sic Viper on her family or drag her into court for a custody battle chilled her to the marrow. Somehow she had to appease Derek before matters got out of hand.

By the time her lunch with her mother and Paige was over, Zoey had made up her mind. She'd pay Derek off one last time. For the good of her family. But this time, she'd make him sign something saying this payment meant he gave up all claim to her baby and would stop making financial demands of her. Finito. Finished. This was it.

Once back in the SUV Gage was borrowing from Elaine, Zoey turned her phone back on and saw the list of missed calls. Twelve of them. Eleven from the number Derek had called from, plus one from Gage.

She called Gage back first, needing to hear his voice and calm herself before negotiating her deal with Derek.

"How was lunch?" Gage said when he answered.

"Good." She leaned her head back on the seat and closed her eyes. *Breathe. Slowly.* "Paige and Mom say hi. We, uh…made plans for Thanksgiving. We're bringing tea, wine and paper products."

"No food?"

She snorted. "My family knows I can't cook, and you know that, too. Paige actually asked me *not* to bring food they'd have to pretend to like."

Gage laughed, and she reveled as the rich, warm sound flowed through her.

"So why'd you have your phone off?"

Scrunching her nose, she rubbed her temple where a tension headache had coiled. "I just... didn't want calls interrupting my lunch."

Because Derek is back, and he's blackmailing me. I feel lost and scared and ashamed. How did I get in this mess? Help me.

For all of a minute, she considered going to the police to report Derek's harassment. But bringing in the cops almost guaranteed her family and Gage would find out about the mess she'd made. She was determined to fix things with Derek by herself, her own way. No more running to her parents or Gage to rescue her. Time to grow up and handle her own messes. Somehow.

If ever she needed to talk to her best friend and figure out what to do, how to untangle herself from this predicament, it was now. She almost spilled the whole ugly situation, but... how could she tell her *husband* she was draining money from their account to buy her ex's cooperation. She choked back the bitter self-condemnation that clogged her throat and focused on what Gage was saying.

"…meaning to ask you about something."

Zoey took a cleansing breath and turned the key in the ignition. School would be getting out soon, and she didn't want to be late to pick up Pet. "Ask away."

"I balanced the checkbook the other night at the station, and the bank shows a one-thousand-dollar withdrawal I didn't make."

Cold dread balled in her gut.

"Do you know anything about that?"

"I…um…" Her heart beat so loudly in her ears that she was sure Gage would hear it. Squeezing the steering wheel with one hand and her phone with the other, Zoey floundered. She'd never lied to Gage before and refused to start now.

But she couldn't tell him the truth. He'd only remind her how Derek had stolen her entire savings, tell her paying him off was a mistake, voice all the reasons she already knew why caving to Derek's threats was wrong. Knowing Gage, he'd go after Derek, confront him. Derek would pick a fight. Things could turn ugly, violent—a habit Gage's father had demonstrated well and Gage had been determined to never repeat.

Or he'd call the police on Derek. Which was as good as throwing gas on the fire, declaring war with her ex and his cronies. Viper might even retaliate, likely doing something to hurt Pet, or Gage, or her parents. Or Derek would sue for custody of her baby out of sheer spite. Or he'd find a way to—

"Zee, you there?" Gage's voice cut into her troubled thoughts.

Zoey swallowed hard. "I withdrew the money."

"Oh. Well...mind if I ask why?"

"I...had to make a p-payment to...something."

"What kind of payment? Like on a credit card?"

"Well, sort of." *No.* "More like...um, insurance." *Ensuring no one tried to come after our family.*

And how did that work out for ya, Zoey? He's back demanding more.

Tears of frustration and guilt puddled in her eyes.

"Insurance?" Gage paused. "Well, why didn't you just write a check? You know mailing cash is really risky."

"Yeah...I— Next time, I will."

Next time. There shouldn't be a next time. And yet she was considering another payment to Derek. *Five thousand dollars or a custody battle.* Zoey placed a trembling hand over her belly, where her baby was growing, and her heart gave a painful throb. She couldn't risk losing her baby. If Derek so much as won visitation rights, he could disappear with her baby and demand huge sums for the baby's safe return.

"So is this insurance a monthly bill? Something I need to work into the budget?" Gage asked.

"No...I—" Guilt pinched Zoey's chest. "It doesn't need to come from the budget. I'll... figure something out."

"Zee? If this is something important, we can find a way to pay for—" Through the phone,

Zoey heard an alarm sound in the background. "Duty calls. Talk to ya later."

Before she could say as much as "Goodbye," he was gone. Zoey flipped the phone closed and imagined Gage racing to put on his bunker gear and hurrying off to fight a fire or extricate an accident victim from a car.

Possibly putting his life on the line.

Her pulse skipped a beat. She'd never considered the inherent dangers of his job. Uncomfortable truths like that were better ignored in her ignorance-is-bliss old life.

But if she were truly going to turn her life around and start taking more responsibility for her actions, she had to face more than a few sobering facts. She had to look at the big picture, not just her own wishes. Instead of her usual impulsiveness, she had to think before she acted. And she had to deal with the reality that her best friend—her husband—ran into burning buildings in the line of duty. She shuddered. What would she ever do if she lost Gage? The empty bleakness was too horrid to ponder.

With a heavy heart, she stashed her phone in

her purse. Of course he'd discovered her withdrawal. Had she really thought he wouldn't notice the missing money?

Insurance. That much hadn't been a total fabrication. Still, her evasiveness knotted tension inside her. When she was back on her feet, she'd repay Gage with interest.

Just that morning she'd stopped by a doctor's office that had advertised needing a receptionist—only to find the position had been filled. Somehow she had to find a job so she could reimburse Gage, pay for her baby and make her own way.

Until then…she had business to settle.

She called Derek, and he answered on the first ring. "Don't ignore me, Zoey!" he growled. "I'm not playing. I need that money, and I will do whatever it takes to get it. Hear me?"

Zoey gritted her teeth. "I couldn't talk before. I—"

"I know where that kid, Gage's kid, goes to school. I can get to her. I'll take her for real this time! How much ransom you think lover boy would pay for the kid?"

Hatred for Derek flowed through her until she shook with fury. "Don't you touch her! I'll get you the damn money!"

Derek was silent.

Zoey pushed past the constriction in her throat. A sour taste filled her mouth. "I don't know where I'll get it or how long it will take, but I'll get it. Somehow."

"All five grand?"

She huffed her disgust. "Yes. But there are conditions."

"Conditions?" Derek scoffed. "You can't lay conditions—"

"Shut up and listen to me, Derek! If you want this money, you will meet *my* demands. Got it?" She jabbed the steering wheel with a finger, then tried futilely to stop the shudders racking her body.

"Fine," he barked, "what?"

"First, this is it. You get no more after this. Zero. I swear if you so much as mention money to me again after this, I'll...sue you for extortion!" An idle threat. She'd never have the guts to drag her family's name through the mud that such a lawsuit would entail. Her entire association with Derek, how he'd used her, stolen from her, gotten her pregnant and abandoned her, would be laid bare in a courtroom. The media would have a field day broadcasting the Bancroft family dirt. She couldn't do that to her parents, her sisters. Her family's company.

Derek grunted in dismissal.

"Second," she continued doggedly, "you will stay away from my family. If anyone in my family so much as hears a peep from you, if one hair on anyone's head is touched, the deal is off. I'll let Viper tear you apart before I let you harm my family."

She took a breath. "Third, you will give up all rights to this child. You will stay away from me and my baby. Permanently."

"Whatever." He sounded bored, patronizing.

She tightened her grip on the steering wheel, ignoring the horn blast of a car behind her, rushing her to vacate the parking space. "And you will sign a statement agreeing to all of these conditions before you see a penny."

"Is that really necessary, Red?"

"Yes! I don't trust you. I want *something* to fall back on, *something* to take to court if you try to pull something else down the road." Derek said nothing for a moment, and Zoey's heart thundered anxiously. "Well?"

"All right!" he snapped. "You get the cash, draw up your freaking statement for me to sign and meet me at the diner by exit 113 off the main highway through Lagniappe. Tonight. Eight o'clock. Got it?"

Her heart jolted. "Tonight? How am I supposed to get the money by tonight?"

"You'll think of something."

"But, Derek—"

A dial tone buzzed in her ear, and her shoulders drooped. She was so preoccupied with figuring out how she could get the money in the next seven hours that she almost missed another chilling detail.

She'd known Derek was in town, but if he was recovering from a beating the night before, that had to mean Viper was in town, too.

Chapter 8

Paige scribbled her signature on the check and ripped it from the book. "So...are you going to tell me what this money is for, or does it fall under the category of it's-almost-Christmas, it's-for-a-secret gift?"

Zoey took the check for two thousand dollars from her sister and jammed it in her pocket. "Um, yeah. Something like that." *If you could call securing peace of mind and our family's safety a Christmas gift.* "Thanks. This means a lot to me. And I'll pay you back as soon as possible. I promise."

Paige shrugged. "I know you're trying to get back on your feet. I wouldn't do this if I weren't sure that you're finally heading in the right direction now, marrying Gage and settling down to have a baby. You need a nest egg of your own to start building your future." Her sister capped her pen, then aimed it at Zoey's pocket with a grin. "Just don't forget where you put the check and let it go through the wash."

Zoey feigned dismay. "I wouldn't do that."

Paige laughed. "Yes, you would. You have before."

"Touché," Zoey groaned.

But she had no intention of letting the check stay in her pocket past that afternoon. As soon as the family finished eating Thanksgiving dinner, she would call Derek and meet him at the diner again. She'd managed to put him off several days, giving him the five thousand in installments. Fifteen hundred dollars last Friday, when she met with him at the diner the first time, another fifteen hundred that she'd gotten as a loan from her mother on Monday. But she knew she was out of time. When she made this last payment, she'd have Derek sign the papers she'd drawn up, her terms for his getting the money, before she passed Paige's check over to him.

She had no idea how she'd repay her mother or Paige...or Gage, for that matter. But she would. Even if she had to take a job as an elf at the mall over Christmas to earn it.

Holly poked her head into the back room where Zoey had dragged Paige for privacy for the transaction. "What's with the secret powwow?"

"If we told you, it wouldn't be a secret, now would it?" Paige gave her sister a smug grin.

Zoey crossed to the door and hooked her arm in Holly's. "Or we could tell you, but then..."

"We'd have to kill you!" the three sisters said at the same time, chuckling.

Holly tightened her grip on Zoey's arm and shuddered. "I think this family has had about enough of secrets that could get us killed. First with my brother-in-law, then Paige's fiancé..."

"Let's make a pact. Nothing but complete honesty for the Bancroft sisters from here on out." Paige put her hand out, and Holly untangled herself from Zoey's grip to stack her hand on top. Zoey's heart tripped, and she hesitated. *Complete honesty.*

More than anything she wished she could be completely honest with her sisters about the dangerous predicament she found herself in. They'd been so close in high school and had the chance now to rebuild that bond as they all forged new beginnings with their husbands.

Holly and Paige turned to her. Waiting. Zoey mentally crossed her fingers behind her back. As soon as she got Derek off her back, as soon as she was sure Viper posed no threat to her family, she swore she'd be honest with her sisters. Forcing a smile, she stacked her hand on her sisters', like a baseball team rallying before a game.

"Honesty!" Paige and Holly chanted.

"Now—" Holly shifted to curve her arms around Paige's and Zoey's shoulders "—I was sent to tell you that dinner was ready."

"Good! I'm starving." Zoey's stomach growled, echoing her claim.

Paige shook her head. "Pregnant people."

"Just you wait until it's your turn!" Holly nudged them forward. "Come on, the kids are helping Mom put food on the table as we speak."

Zoey's eyes widened. "She's letting Pet near the stove? Near china? Is she crazy?"

Holly laughed. "I think Pet was given the bread basket and the silverware."

Arm in arm, the three headed toward the dining room, Holly waddling with her eight-months-pregnant belly and Zoey tamping down the impulse to race to the kitchen in fear of a Pet-caused disaster. Instead, Pet and Holly's two stepchildren, Miles and Palmer, were already seated at a card table in an area adjoining the dining room where the adults were eating.

Neil led the family in a prayer of Thanksgiving, mentioning how grateful he was to have his whole family gathered around him this year.

Zoey peeked at the faces around the table as her father prayed, and a knot of emotion clogged her throat. She loved these people, her family. Even Paige's new husband, Jake, whom she'd met only a couple of months ago when she got back to town.

Jake made Paige happier than she'd ever seen her sister, and Zoey found him charming and easy to talk to. And Matt was Holly's second chance for true love and family, after tragedy stole her first husband. Even without being pregnant, Holly would have been glowing with bliss for the new family in her life. Her sisters had both been through dangerous and emotional turmoil in recent months, and knowing how close she'd come to losing both of them caused a shiver to chase down her spine.

Her parents had been stalwarts of love and patience with her throughout her turbulent teen years, and the innocent children around the card table brought a new joy to her life. And Gage... where did she begin?

She thought about the check in her pocket, and her chest tightened. These were the people she was protecting. Her mistakes had caused her parents, her sisters and Gage enough grief for one lifetime. She'd do *anything* she must to spare them any more trouble, any more danger and more sleepless nights.

"Amen." The chorus of voices around her brought Zoey from her drifting thoughts.

"It all looks fabulous, ladies," Jake said, helping himself to the corn bread dressing in front of him.

The kids brought their plates in to be served, and bowls and platters started circulating, while Neil carved the turkey.

"How's that new security firm doing, Jake?" Gage asked as he scooped sweet potatoes onto Pet's plate. When Pet wrinkled her nose, he whispered, "Try it, please. Look, it has marshmallows on top. It tastes kinda like pumpkin pie."

"We're off to a good start," Jake answered. "And I couldn't ask for a more organized or creatively ambitious office manager." He smiled at Paige, whose cheeks pinkened.

Matt updated the family on the new grant he'd received to run the low-cost health clinic in Morgan Hollow, North Carolina, where he and Holly lived. "And the county hospital has asked me to be the pediatric doctor for their emergency room. The extra income will be nice, especially since Holly won't be teaching after the baby comes."

"Dad, Paige tells me you're thinking of taking early retirement from Bancroft Industries next year," Jake said as he shoveled turkey onto his fork. "What made you decide to do that?"

"Five reasons," Neil replied, "Namely Palmer, Miles, Pet, and Holly's and Zoey's babies. I want to enjoy my grandkids, take them to Disney World, spoil them while they're young."

"Did he say we're going to Disney World?" Miles called from the next room, his tone full of enthusiasm and hopeful excitement. The adults laughed.

"So he *can* hear," Holly said with a chuckle. "I'd have sworn he was deaf. When he's playing his with his DS, there's no way to get his attention."

"It's called selective hearing." Ellen smiled and pointed her fork at Holly. "It affects all children. You were that way about your Barbies."

"Really? I thought Zoey was the one who

always had her head in the clouds." Holly lifted the cloth on the bread basket and frowned. "Oops. We're out of rolls."

"There are more in the oven. They should be ready," Ellen said, scooting her chair back.

"Sit," Matt said with a warm smile. "I'll get the rolls. You've been on your feet all morning." He pushed his chair back and disappeared into the kitchen.

Leaning her chair back slightly, Zoey used the break in the conversation to peek into the next room to check on Pet. Gage's niece giggled at something Miles said, her plate nearly empty. No spills. No disasters. *Yet.*

Suddenly Holly grabbed Zoey's wrist and squeezed. Hard.

"Ow!" Zoey dropped the front legs of her chair to the floor and whipped her attention to her sister. "What the—"

The grimace of pain on Holly's face, the wan color of her complexion, stopped Zoey midsentence. No one else seemed to notice. Conversations continued. Laughter rippled around the table. Forks clinked on bone china.

Zoey closed her hand over her sister's viselike grip and leaned close. "Hol? What is it?"

"A contraction," her sister rasped. "I've been... having mild ones...all day. Braxton Hicks. But that one—" Holly gasped. Bit her lip. Shot a terrified look at Zoey.

Zoey's heart thundered in her chest. "What? What!"

"My water broke!" Holly cringed, clearly in the midst of another painful contraction.

Panic swelled in Zoey's throat. "But...it's too soon!"

Holly pulled a no-shit-Sherlock face. "I know!"

Zoey shoved her chair back, her hands fluttering nervously. "We gotta get you to the hospital."

"Ya think?" Holly groaned.

The rest of the family had now taken notice of the sisters' hushed but anxious exchange. Concerned looks and quiet inquiries clambered at the edges of Zoey's attention, but her focus was on her sister. Do something!

"Matt!" she yelled as she help Holly to her feet, "Forget the rolls! Get the car!"

Matt poked his head in from the next room. "What are you—" When he saw his wife, doubled over in pain, blood and amniotic fluid covering her legs, he blanched and darted to her side. "Holly!"

"We have to get her to the hospital." Zoey's voice cracked, worry for her sister choking her. "She's in premature labor!"

Gage tried to concentrate on the children's book Pet had picked for him to read at the hospital as they waited for news about Holly and the baby, but his focus strayed every time a doctor walked past or an alarm beeped behind the nurses' desk. A voice over the intercom announced some color-coded emergency, and he and the rest of Zoey's family jerked to attention.

Ellen huddled against Neil, looking shell-shocked. Jake paced, while Paige tried to distract Matt's children with a puzzle book. Pet seemed agitated, aware that something was wrong, but mostly put out that they'd left the house before dessert.

Beside him, Zoey fidgeted, drumming her fingers and twisting the loose ends of her sweater's belt. He wished he could do something to ease the tension pulsing in the room. He cared deeply for the Bancrofts, who had been more of a family to him since junior high than his blood relatives had. Sitting around the Thanksgiving table today, he hadn't been the outsider this family included out of kindness. He'd *belonged*.

As Zoey's husband, he was a *real* member of the family. As they'd given thanks at dinner for the blessings in their lives, familial love and contentment had washed over him, filling his chest until he couldn't breathe. Now a shared concern for his sister-in-law and her baby sat like a rock on his heart. Gage read the next few lines of the book, then cast another anxious glance around the waiting room.

When Zoey surged to her feet and stalked toward the vending machine at the far end of the hall, Gage scooted Pet from his lap and handed Paige the storybook.

"Would you mind keeping an eye on Pet for a minute?"

Paige glanced down the corridor to her youngest sister and nodded. "Zoey's never been good in a crisis. She gets so emotional, overreacts." She twitched a wry smile. "But I guess you know that, don't you?"

"Yeah." Gage rolled his shoulders. "But I think the depth of her feelings in all things, not just crisis, is one of the reasons I love her. For a long time, I drifted through life anesthetized and detached because my reality was too ugly."

Compassion filled Paige's eyes. "Because of your parents. I remember." She hitched her head toward her sister. "Go. Pet will be fine with me."

Smiling his thanks, Gage strode toward Zoey, who stared blankly at the candy machine.

"Want something?" He jangled the coins in his pocket. "I think I have enough change."

"Huh?" She lifted a bewildered look that

confirmed that she wasn't perusing the snack options, so much as she was lost in turbulent thoughts.

He tipped his head in query. "You okay?"

She hesitated and frowned, as if taking a mental inventory. "No." Her chin quivered. "I'm scared. What if something happens to Holly? Or her baby?"

He opened his arms, offering her a hug that she ignored. Or didn't register. Her gaze looked distant, preoccupied. "They'll be fine. You have to believe that. Stay positive."

"I'm trying to, but…" She crossed her arms, clutching her elbows, and shivered.

Gage stepped closer, wrapping her in the hug she clearly needed. He tucked her head under his chin and rubbed her back. Holding her made it harder to keep the emotional distance he needed with Zoey, especially in light of the family's crisis. He'd just become part of this family, and the idea that he could lose any of them so quickly and without warning shook him to the core—proof enough he needed to do a better job guarding his heart.

"Sh-she took such good care of herself...her whole pregnancy." Zoey's voice cracked, and her fingers dug into his shirt. "She did e-everything right. How could this h-happen?" Pushing to arm's length from him, Zoey raised green eyes, bright with tears and alarm. "If this could happen to Holly, when she was so careful, what chance do I have? What if something happens to my baby, Gage? I—I—"

"Your baby is going to be fine. And so is your sister's." His throat squeezing with emotion, he tugged her close and buried his face in the thick waves of her hair. Her continued reference to the baby as *hers* instead of *theirs* rubbed salt in his wounded soul. In so many small ways, she told him they weren't a *real* couple and never would be.

By turning her back to him as she slept. By offering her cheek when he wanted to kiss her goodbye in the morning. By keeping secrets from him.

He knew something had been bothering her for days, yet she changed the subject when he tried to ask her about it. Her vagueness about the thousand-dollar withdrawal told him she saw her business as her own and not something to share. He hadn't badgered her about the money, but he'd been left with more questions than answers and an increasing sense of distance between them.

Today he'd felt closer to the Bancrofts, more a part of their family than ever before, while his eleven-year relationship with Zoey seemed to be fraying at the ends, coming apart at the seams. Was their marriage the beginning of the end of their friendship? He didn't want to believe it, yet he felt Zoey slipping away from him.

An empty ache lodged in his chest, and he squeezed Zoey tighter, inhaling the familiar fruity scent of her shampoo and trying to convince himself he could salvage their friendship and still protect his heart.

He held her, letting her sniffle and cling for several minutes, until he saw Matt emerge from the delivery room at the other end of the corridor. Matt wore a grave expression and walked with sagging shoulders, as if he carried a great weight.

Gage tensed, and clearly sensing the change in him, Zoey pulled away, raised a wary look. He nodded toward the far end of the hall. "Matt's coming."

She gasped and hurried to intercept her brother-in-law. When her family saw her whiz past the waiting room, they, too, rose to meet Matt halfway.

Zoey reached him first, battering him with questions. "Well? What did the doctor say? How's Holly?"

He raised a quieting hand and inhaled deeply, sending an encompassing glance to all of the family. "Holly is fine, but...they couldn't stop the labor." Matt gave them a bittersweet smile. "We have a son. Adam Neil."

Miles and Palmer scurried up to their father and clutched his legs. He lifted six-year-old Miles into his arms for a bear hug.

Joyous coos and sighs of relief surrounded Gage, but he read the hesitation in his brother-in-law's eyes. "But?"

Matt met Gage's gaze with darkly worried eyes. "But he's underweight, obviously..." He stopped to clear the thickness from his voice. "...since he's five weeks early. Three pounds and twelve ounces." Moisture filled Matt's eyes. "He's on a respirator. It's still touch-and-go."

Gage's stomach sank. With a stifled sob, Zoey threw her arms around Matt, including Miles in her embrace.

Jake draped his arm over Paige's shoulders and drew her close, kissing her temple as her face crumpled with distress.

Pet, who'd been holding Paige's hand, sidled over to grab Gage's hand now, her expression cautious and curious.

"Can we see Holly?" Ellen asked. "She shouldn't be alone now."

Matt nodded. "They're moving her to her room. I just wanted to let you know...before I joined her."

Paige raised her head from Jake's shoulder. "What about Adam? He shouldn't be alone, either. Will they let one of us sit with him in the PICU?"

Matt pulled away from Zoey, swiping at

his eyes and nodding. "Only two at a time, though."

"Let me go," Zoey said. Knitting her brow, she slid a hand over the tiny bump of her lower abdomen. "Please. I need—" She bit her lip without finishing the thought, then faced her sister. "Paige, will you go with me?"

Paige pulled free of her husband and took Zoey's hand, nodding. "Of course."

Gage bit down on the selfish disappointment that kicked his gut when Zoey asked her sister to join her vigil over her nephew instead of him. Paige had every right, more right than he had, to be at the baby's side. But Zoey's preference for her sister's company felt like a snub. More distance. Another thread pulled from the fabric of their relationship.

Neil squared his shoulders, projecting fatherly authority, despite the lines of fatigue and worry etched in his face. "All right, then. Ellen, Matt and I will sit with Holly. Paige and Zoey will be in PICU with Adam." He turned to Jake and Gage. "Do you guys mind watching the kids?

You can take them back to the house where they won't be so bored."

Pet tugged his arm. "Can we go home and have pie now?"

"Now there's a girl with a good idea." Jake, clearly trying to sound cheerful for the children's sake, took Miles from Matt. "What do ya say we go have some pie to celebrate your new brother?"

Miles gave his father an uneasy look, and Matt ruffled his hair. "It's okay, sport. I'll come home later and check on you."

Gage understood Miles's reluctance to leave the hospital. He didn't want to leave with Zoey still so upset. He wanted to be her support, her confidant through this family emergency. Like she'd been for him so many times in high school.

Paige gave Jake a kiss before he left. "Thanks, honey. I'll be home to help you later. Soon we'll work out a visitation schedule for who goes where that works for everyone."

Gage stepped closer to Zoey. "Are you sure

you don't want me to stay with you? I can call Rani to help babysit the kids."

Zoey shook her head, a frown pocking her brow. "It's Thanksgiving. Don't pull Rani away from her family. I'll be fine. I think Pet needs you now more than I do."

Right. Of course. His five-year-old niece needed him more than Zoey who had her whole family around her.

Sighing his acceptance, Gage gave Zoey a peck on the cheek, then followed Jake and the kids out to the parking garage. All he could do now was be patient. Experience had taught him that if he pushed Zoey too hard, she would get spooked, and more stress was the last thing she needed now.

Chapter 9

Around 1:00 a.m. that night, Zoey keyed open the door to Gage's house and stumbled into the kitchen. Her heart, burdened with images of her tiny nephew fighting for his life, sat like a paperweight in her chest, while her mind spun like a carnival ride.

Without turning on the overhead light, she groped her way to the refrigerator and took out the milk. In the glow from the open appliance, she poured herself a tall glass and drank half of it without stopping.

"I wasn't expecting you home tonight."

The overhead light flicked on, and sloshing the remaining milk on her shirt, she spun with a gasp to face Gage. "Leapin' lizards, you startled me!"

"Sorry, but why were you creeping around in the dark?"

She mopped ineffectively at the milk on her blouse with tissue from her pocket and frowned. "I didn't want the lights to wake you."

"I wasn't asleep. Too much on my mind." Gage pulled a hand towel from a drawer and tossed it to her. "I thought you were staying the night at the hospital."

"I would have, but Mom and Dad made me come home to rest. They're worried about me overdoing it and jeopardizing my baby."

"Good for them. I was a little concerned about that, too."

She yawned and sopped moisture from her clothes. "After Holly fell asleep, Mom took the sleeper chair by the hospital bed, and Matt and Dad went upstairs to be with the baby. Paige went back to Mom and Dad's house to relieve Jake of babysitting duty and to get some sleep."

Her head nodded, heavy with fatigue, and she blinked herself awake. As physically exhausted as she was, she doubted her spinning thoughts, her guilt about Derek's extortion, her concern for baby Adam, would allow her to sleep.

Her contacts felt gritty and dry, after too many hours of wear and the drying air of the hospital's heating system. She plucked a contacts case from her purse and used the reflective surface of the microwave door to see as she took out her contacts.

"I brought Pet home around ten," Gage said. "She was asleep before her head hit the pillow."

"I know how she feels." Zoey yawned. Her glasses were back in the master bathroom, so she squinted to clear the fuzzy images around her.

The damp fabric of her shirt caused a shiver to race over her skin. Knowing the milk would stink if not washed out soon, she started unbuttoning her blouse. "We'll change shifts again in the morning, giving Matt, Mom and Dad a chance to sleep and shower."

"I'm happy to do whatever your family needs me to do. Watch the kids, run errands, sit with Holly—" Gage stopped abruptly when she peeled her blouse off her shoulders and wadded it into a ball. A choking sound gurgled from his throat.

She tipped her head in query. "You all right?"

He rubbed his face and averted his gaze. "Sure. I just…" His hand flailed in a vague gesture that meant nothing to her.

Shaking her head, she headed into the laundry room. "Let me just start this wash before the milk stinks, then I'm going to bed." Zoey dumped the shirt into the machine with the towel and uncapped the detergent. She tried to read the directions on the box, but without her contacts, the letters blurred. "How much of this you figure I should use for one shirt and one towel?"

Gage stepped up behind her and took the laundry soap from her. "Just a little. And I wouldn't wash the shirt and towel together."

"Why not?" she asked automatically, although at this point, she didn't care. She couldn't get the hissing sound of Adam's respirator out of her head. What did laundry matter when her nephew was struggling for each breath?

A sob welled in her throat, and she swallowed hard to force it down. She'd been on the edge of tears all day, a condition she attributed as much to pregnancy hormones as Adam's precarious condition. These days, even jewelry stores' Christmas commercials or running out of Pet's favorite cereal made her cry. Stupid hormones.

Gage reached around her from behind, his chest bumping her nearly naked back as he pulled the towel out of the washer tub. "Because your shirt is a bright color and should be washed on cold. I wash towels on hot to kill germs."

Heat from his body chased the chill that had settled in her bones at the hospital and resided there ever since. Without thinking about it, she rocked back on her heels and leaned against his broad chest. She needed his strength and support now more than ever. And not just because she was swaying on her feet with fatigue. "When did you learn to wash clothes?"

His fingers wrapped around her shoulder, steadying her, burning imprints on her bare skin. "Long time ago. It only takes a few goof-ups before you learn how to separate loads."

Goof-ups. The word jumped out at her, wagging an accusing finger.

More tears, born of exhaustion and egged on by pregnancy hormones and stress, pricked her eyes. "I'm so tired of goofing up." Her voice cracked, but she didn't bother hiding her distress. "Even when I try to do the right thing, it turns out wrong."

Gage sighed and laid his arm along her collarbone in a backward hug. "Zee, I wasn't criticizing. Please don't cry. It wouldn't hurt the towel to wash it on cold, I just—"

"I don't mean the stupid laundry." She pivoted in the space between his body and the washer and shook her head. Curling her fingers into the T-shirt he wore with his sleep pants, she sniffed back the moisture burning her sinuses. "Although there is that, *too*."

Zoey rested her forehead on his chest with a groan. "I've done nothing but make mistakes and hurt people for years now. Starting with how I hurt you when I ran off to Europe six years ago. But if I'm trying to do the right thing, why does everything keep backfiring on me? Why do I keep screwing everything up?"

Gage hugged her closer and propped his chin on top of her head. "What brought this on? You're not screwing anything up now."

She tensed, and a whimper escaped her throat. *Except that I'm letting my ex-boyfriend extort money I don't have to keep my family safe.*

"And I'm not saying you were a screwup before," he said, rubbing her back and clearly misinterpreting her response. "I'm just using your words."

Zoey squeezed her eyes closed. Keeping Derek's extortion from Gage was tearing her up inside. She hated having a secret she couldn't share with Gage. Her silence felt like the first brick in a wall that would separate her from

Gage and ruin the closeness they'd shared for years.

So tell him!

She clenched her teeth and forced down the bitter taste in her throat.

*No...*she couldn't tell Gage. Not yet. He'd try to stop her from caving to Derek's demands, putting himself in danger. He'd try to "fix" things for her, the way he did when he'd convinced her to marry him. He'd already put enough of his life on hold for her. And she was ready, *determined* to fix this problem herself. She didn't want Gage or her parents or her sisters bailing her out of trouble again. She had to make a stand for herself.

"Zee, what's wrong? What's going on with you?" Gage stroked her hair, his voice low and comforting. "You've been distracted and edgy for weeks. Talk to me."

She shook her head and tried to pull away from his grip. "It's nothing."

"Zee?"

She unfastened her jeans, blinking back the sting of tears and toeing off her shoes, then shoved the denim pants down her legs. "Might as w-well wash these with the blouse. No point wasting w-water."

Gage inhaled sharply and stepped back. "Geez, Zee, you're killing me..."

She gave him a puzzled look, and he waved a hand at her dishabille.

Turning to shove the jeans into the washing machine, she rolled her eyes. "How many times have you seen me in a bikini at my parents' pool? I'm just as covered now as when I wear my bikini."

"You don't think your bikini turns me on?"

Zoey grunted. "It shouldn't. Normally I'm as straight and flat as a board. And now...well, this baby bump is hardly sexy."

He mumbled something under his breath that sounded like "That's what you think."

Her baby-swollen belly turned Gage on? The thought was...unsettling. Intriguing. Breath-stealing.

As she submerged the jeans in the washer tub, she remembered Paige's check in her pocket. Snatching the pants back out, she retrieved the last installment of money for Derek. Water had spotted it, but not beyond salvaging.

She'd planned to give the money to him this afternoon, before Holly had headed to the hospital. Her stomach churned when she considered what Derek or Viper might do to retaliate for her missed payment deadline.

"What's that?" Gage asked.

Her heart thumped a panicked rhythm. She hid the check behind her back and ducked her chin, avoiding his eyes. "Um…it's from Paige. I—" Her excuse stuck in her throat, when, with her gaze lowered, she noticed that Gage was… well, *hard*.

That's what you think.

She blinked a couple times, wondering if her contactless, blurred vision was deceiving her. But no, he was definitely *aroused*. Because she was in her bra and panties? Okay, that freaked her out.

"You know…" She cleared her throat and fumbled to refocus her thoughts away from Gage's— Leapin' lizards! "I'm…allowed a few secrets before Christmas. You wouldn't want to spoil a surprise, would you?"

He arched an eyebrow, signaling his skepticism. "Whatever."

"Now..." She slid between Gage and the wall, trying not to brush up against him and his... oh, boy! "If you'll excuse me..." She padded into the kitchen and shoved the check in a front pocket of her purse. She heard the shuffle of feet, telling her Gage had followed her from the laundry room.

Her head spun—with fatigue, with worry for Adam, with anxiety over Derek's manipulation and with...shock. Gage had a hard-on...for *her?* It was too much. The day's tumultuous events swirled together in a confusing, upsetting kaleidoscope of color and emotion. The room seemed to tilt, and she gripped the edge of the kitchen counter to steady herself. The tears she'd been battling since she arrived home surged forward in a kamikaze-style attack on her senses. A sob wrenched from her chest, and her knees buckled. As she wilted, strong arms grabbed her and hauled her into a firm embrace.

"Aw, Zee…" Gage scooped her up and carried her to the living room sofa, where he set her gently on the cushions. Settling next to her, he pulled her head down to his shoulder. "Let it out. I know it's been a tough day."

"If Adam dies—" she cried.

"He won't."

"He could!"

"Don't think that way, Zee."

"I can't help it. I'm scared. For Holly and Matt…and f-for our baby. What if something terrible hap—"

Gage jerked, sucking in a shallow breath and tightening his hold.

Zoey peered up at him, squinting at the contacts-free image, and fresh fear streaking through her. "What?"

The corner of his mouth twitched. "You said *our* baby. That's the first time you ever called it *ours*." His smile brightening, he swiped her cheek with a thumb, then pressed a kiss to her forehead. "Thank you."

"I didn't realize…I mean— It really matters *that much* to you?"

He moved his soft kiss to her cheek, his stubbled chin lightly scraping her skin. "Yes. Because *you* mean that much to me, Zee."

Her heart gave a bittersweet throb. His response was the sweet kind he had a knack for, the kind that reminded her of all the reasons he was her friend. And yet...

The hypnotic stroke of his fingers on her face, the heat in his eyes and the tingles that raced through her when his lips brushed her face... seduced her. In the shadowed living room, with his chin covered in late-night beard and his espresso eyes hooded with intensity and desire, Zoey could almost forget that this was her best friend, not a potential lover.

It would be so easy to lose herself for a few blissful moments in the paradise his body offered. She remembered well how earthshaking making love to Gage could be, how mind-numbingly moving, how deeply powerful...

Despite her no-sex rule, she curled her fingers into his hair and raised her lips to his. She was too tired tonight to fight temptation, too emotional to stop and second-guess the impulse urging her on.

The warmth of his mouth and tug of his kiss stole her breath. When he groaned his approval and greeted her tongue with his own, a ripple of sensation, like sparks from a live wire, spun through her.

Rather than object when he laid her back on the couch, her body clamored to be closer to him. He stretched beside her, wedging her between the back of the sofa and his broad chest, and the soft cotton of his night clothes gently abraded her exposed skin. He skimmed a hand up her bare leg, over her hip, and settled on the baby bump at her belly. His fingers splayed over the spot where her baby—*their* baby—was growing, and the tenderness of the gesture sent more moisture to her eyes. Derek may have donated the sperm, but Gage *wanted* her baby. And she wanted to make Gage happy, wanted to share the miracle of her child with him. In that moment she knew a completeness, a security and joy that enveloped her with warmth. She was with Gage, and she was safe.

But seconds later, Gage shifted his hand to the dip at her waist before moving upward, setting fires with his sensual touch. When his fingers reached the clasp of her bra, he hesitated.

Zoey whimpered her disappointment. She didn't want to think, to hesitate. Right now she needed to lose herself in sensation more than she needed caution. She wanted escape more than the restraints of reality. She wanted the sexual completion her body hungered for like oxygen.

She quashed his doubts by hooking her leg around his hip and sliding a hand down his back to sink her fingers into one buttock. With their bodies pressed close, he manipulated the back hook of her bra, and her nipples puckered in anticipation, aching for his touch.

Once he had the lacy demi cups unfastened, Gage tugged the silky garment out of his way. His gaze devoured her while his palm cupped first one breast, then the other, teasing the budded peak with a flick of his thumb. Lightning bolts of pleasure shot straight to her core, and she writhed against him. Grabbing a fistful of fabric, she yanked his T-shirt over his head and dropped it on the floor.

He levered back from her, his dark eyes searching hers, his breath coming in short shallow pants. "Touch me, Zee. I want to feel your hands on me," he rasped.

His need fanned the fire in her, and with hands shaking with eager desire, she explored his chest, the dark hair surrounding his navel, and…lower. Inside his sleep pants. When she wrapped her fingers around his steely length, Gage's hips bucked off the sofa, and a guttural groan ripped from his throat.

Zoey caught the rumble of satisfaction with a deep kiss, and he anchored her head between his hands, making love to her mouth with his lips and tongue. Claiming her. Branding her.

She slid her arms around his back, clutching at him with the same edge of desperation that colored his kiss. Her body wept for a reward just beyond reach, while wispy memories taunted her, drifting like smoke through her mind.

Gage insinuated a hand between her legs and skillfully caressed her tender flesh, tantalizing her. When he slid a finger inside her, she nearly shattered.

But a vague warning whispered in her ear, confusing her, distracting her, and she struggled to shut out the nagging alarm that left her off balance. Like a thirsty soul crawling toward a mirage in the desert, Zoey reached, hands groping, for the nirvana her body craved, but a heavy sadness settled in her chest, held her back, filled her with an anguish she couldn't exorcize.

The incongruence frustrated her, frightened her. She remembered this same terrifying feeling washing through her the morning after graduation. The morning after she'd given her virginity to Gage. The morning she'd broken Gage's heart...

What was she *doing?* How could she jeopardize their friendship for a few minutes of pleasure?

Tears flooded her sinuses and spilled onto her cheeks. "No..." Her moan welled up from the stinging ache in her heart. She shoved at his shoulders and clamped her legs together. "Noooo."

Gage moved his hand away from her legs but still held her close, kissing her throat, nuzzling her ear. "What do you want, babe? Name it."

She tried to clear her mind, to verbalize the doubts that tormented her, but he seized her lips with another deep lingering kiss.

"I want to get inside you," he murmured huskily. "I've waited so long…" he kissed her again "…but you're worth the wait."

An echo from the past blasted Zoey's brain, and pain slashed through her. "Stop!"

She wrenched free of him, shoving his chest so hard he rolled off the sofa, thumping to the floor. He raised a dazed look to her as he sat up. "Zee?"

Zoey buried her face in her hands, and deep, heaving sobs wracked her body. "I—I can't… d-do this."

The sofa sagged beside her as he sat down, and he stroked her hair, her arm. "Because of the baby? Did your doctor tell you not to—"

"No. No!"

"Shh, keep your voice down. We don't want to wake Pet." He reached for her, but she twisted away from his touch and lunged to her feet. "If not the baby, then…why?"

She shook her head and raised her tear-blurred gaze to him. "Because it's *you*. I can't—I c-can't—" She floundered, trying to understand her own tangled feelings and make sense of the pounding regret that made her stop the best sex of her life. "You p-promised no sex. It was one of m-my conditions for m-marrying you."

Shadows filled Gage's face, and his brow furrowed in confusion. "I thought—" He clenched his jaw and dragged a hand over his mouth. "*You* kissed *me*. You pulled my shirt off and… and wrapped your legs around me, and…" His tone sharpened with his frustration. "You… were wet and ready. You…you can't tell me you didn't want it!" He shoved to his feet and aimed a finger at her. "You made the first move."

"I know! And it was a mistake!" She snatched the quilt from the back of the couch and wrapped it around her shivering body. "A huge mistake." She slapped angrily at the tears pouring down her cheeks. "Do you want to tell me *now* I'm not a screwup? I almost repeated the worst blunder of my life just now. What kind of idiot does that make me, if I don't learn from my mistakes?"

Gage grew eerily still. "Worst blunder of your life?"

"Yes! Sleeping with you, having sex with you the first time was stupid and reckless. But this—" She waved a hand toward the sofa. "This was inexcusable."

He stared at her, his eyes hollow. "Because it was with me."

Something in his voice needled her, waved a red flag. But her own confusion and rampaging grief stampeded over the niggling sensation. "Yes! It's all wrong. Completely, totally *wrong*."

"Didn't feel wrong to me," he said in a low voice.

Zoey tightened the quilt around her and slumped back down on the sofa. "I don't know what I was thinking. I was…tired. And scared. And feeling all emotional because of hormones and stress."

Gage bent his head, lowered his gaze to

the floor and muttered a curse. "You were vulnerable."

"Yeah, I guess. Otherwise, I'd have never—" Lifting her head, she raked hair back from her face and studied Gage's posture, stared at the broad shoulders and muscled chest that had fueled her passion moments ago. If she were honest, she still vibrated with a sexual tension she wished Gage would help her sate.

He looked so handsome, so sexy with his dark hair ruffled from her fingers, his sleep pants riding low on his hips, his warm chest bare and still so tempting.

She groaned. "Jeez, Gage. We're supposed to be *friends*. Best friends. We can't sleep together and not ruin the balance that—"

"You're right, Zoey," he interrupted. "I broke my promise to you. Worse, I took advantage of you when you were vulnerable, and I'm sorry." He paused, and his throat worked as he swallowed hard. "From now until you decide this marriage…this *arrangement* is over, you won't have to worry about me…crossing the line again."

He sucked in a deep breath, and in the dim light of the living room, she'd have sworn he was fighting not to cry. Her heart kicked. She'd only seen him this upset a couple of times—when his father had beaten his mother within an inch of her life their sophomore year and when Gage had fought back and struck his father on graduation night. She absorbed the agony in his voice, in his posture, and a chill slithered through her.

"You want our relationship to be strictly platonic. I get that. I do." He raised his palms to her as if in surrender, as if warning her away.

That gesture alone spoke volumes, but it was his eyes that ripped out a piece of her soul. His gaze was bleak, lost, hurting. Broken.

"Gage…" she whispered, the word raw and rough. She stood and took a step toward him, but he retreated one step in return.

"You can have the bed tonight. You need to rest, to take care of your baby."

As he stalked out of the room, his wording slammed into her as if he'd punched her in the gut. *Your* baby.

Maybe he'd just said it because he was mad. Maybe it didn't reflect how he really felt. Maybe...

Zoey dropped weakly to the couch, staring at nothing, her chest so tight with grief she couldn't breathe.

And maybe her confused feelings for Gage and her reckless sexual advances had cost her the most important person in her life.

Chapter 10

Truth was a bitter pill to swallow. Zoey. Didn't. Want. Him.

Period. Why couldn't he get that through his stupid-assed brain?

Gage snatched his pillow off the bed with a grip so hard that he half expected to see it rip open, sending feathers flying across the bedroom. He ground his back teeth until his jaw throbbed, until he thought a molar might crack.

Graduation night had given him hope that someday Zoey's feeling would change and she'd see him the way he saw her—as a soul mate. But like some freaking schoolboy with a crush, he'd been harboring a fantasy for more than six years. How sad was that?

The sooner he put his crazy notions of building some fairy-tale life with her out of his head, the better off they'd both be.

Because she viewed having sex with him as the biggest blunder of her life. The biggest *blunder* of her life.

Holy crap, Powell! Do you need a tiller rig to hit you to get it through your thick skull? Zoey doesn't love you. She doesn't want to make love with you. And she sure as hell didn't need you jumping her bones tonight when she was hurting and scared and vulnerable.

Gage smacked the wall with the flat of his hand and bit out a curse. Better he give vent to his anger at himself than acknowledge how deeply her rejection hurt. Or face the reality that his unrequited feelings sliced him to the marrow. Or admit that, even after she'd shut him down with her vehemence that sex with *him* was *wrong* and objectionable and, apparently, completely insufferable, his body still ached for her.

She was right about one thing. Their sofa sex had been inexcusable.

He'd been an ass. He'd taken advantage of her, leaping at the first hint that she returned his feelings like the pathetic sap he was.

His best friend had needed comfort and reassurance tonight, and he'd blown it. Sure, she'd made the first move, kissing him. But he knew Zee well enough to know what she'd really needed was someone to hold her, someone to anchor her after what had been a turbulent day, someone to tell her she wasn't alone, no matter how dark life got. Instead he'd groped her, pressured her, *scared her away*.

The morning after graduation, part two.

The image of her sitting wrapped in the quilt, shaking, her eyes bereft, clawed his conscience. His gut twisted with remorse when he thought of all the times in high school he'd been the one at his wit's end, lost and alone because his family was such a nightmare, and Zoey had dropped everything to be his sounding board, his confidant, his beacon through the hell his life had been. And this was how he repaid her?

"Gage?"

When her trembling voice drifted to him from the bedroom door, he tensed. "I'll be out of your way in a second."

He pulled a blanket off the foot of the bed and avoided her gaze as he took his cell phone from his dresser and headed to the couch.

"Where are you going?" She sounded scared, brokenhearted. Ordinarily, he'd be at her side in a second, offering her a hug and a shoulder to cry on. But tonight, right now—hell, maybe from now on—he needed to stay away from her.

"I'll be on the sofa. The bed's all yours."

Her wounded sigh reverberated inside him. "You don't have to—"

"Yeah. Actually, I do." He stopped at the threshold, waiting for her to step out of his way. "I can't be around you tonight." Then realizing how harsh that sounded, he puffed out a short breath. "I just...need to be alone right now."

He hazarded a glance at her face and found

her chin quivering, her cheeks wet and blotchy. His heart twisted.

"Gage, don't…don't pull away like this. I—"

She raised a hand toward his chest, but before she could touch him, Gage shifted the pillow in front of him like a shield and brushed past her into the hall.

When he'd raced off to Nevada to find Zoey, to rescue her from her latest crisis, he'd thought Fate had finally rewarded him for his patience. He'd thought marrying her was the first step toward showing her how good a life together could be, making her fall in love with him.

He'd been ten kinds of foolish.

Only three months into their marriage, and already everything he'd hoped for was crashing around him. He wasn't sure if his friendship with Zoey would survive.

Or if he even wanted it to.

Being the unrequited half of a one-sided love affair hurt too damn much. As important as her friendship was, he had to protect himself, his heart. He needed to put Zoey behind him and find someone who could love him as much as he loved her. He wanted to have a family, he wanted someone he could come home to, make love to, give his heart and soul to without worrying about crossing a line and having her run away from him.

In the eleven years he'd known her, Zoey's feelings for him hadn't changed. Maybe it was time *he* made a change.

He'd made a commitment to Zoey to give her baby a name, to protect her reputation for her family's sake. But once her baby came, he had to do the right thing and free Zoey from their marriage of convenience before it killed what was left of their friendship.

Until then, he had to rein in his feelings for her, keep his hands to himself and find a way to move on with his future—a future that didn't include growing old with his best friend as his wife.

"Where the hell were you yesterday?" Derek glared at Zoey from across the diner table the next afternoon.

"At the hospital. We had a family emergency."

Zoey's head throbbed from lack of sleep and worry, and she was in no mood for a lecture from Derek about what her being late with the money cost him. She gave his fresh set of bruises a guilty glance, then averted her eyes.

"Yeah, well, I had my own emergency, thanks to you. Viper's out for blood," he snarled.

She had enough problems without adding Derek's latest beating from Viper's thugs to the mix. He'd brought this on himself.

Fishing the crumpled check from Paige out of her pocket, she endorsed it and slid it across the table. "The last two thousand. That's it. I'm done." He reached for the check, and she snatched it back. "Not so fast. First…" she slid her document stating he gave up all parental rights to her baby across the sticky Formica "… sign this."

He furrowed his brow and read the simple statements in bold type. "I ain't signing that."

Her gut clenched. "But you said—"

He flashed a reptilian smile and crooked a finger. "Gimme the check."

"Sign." She took out a pen and slapped it on top of the paper.

"After I have my money."

She gritted her teeth, biting back the urge to scream at him that it was her money, her family's money and that he could go jump in a lake.

But the light in Gage's eyes last night when she'd referred to the baby as "theirs," the darkness that filled his expression when she'd stopped him from making love to her, the hurt he'd still worn etched in his brow this morning replayed in her mind's eye. She had to have this assurance from Derek that he wouldn't interfere with the baby, wouldn't try to take away this gift she could give Gage, wouldn't spoil this miracle they could share...if Gage could find a way to forgive her for all the pain she'd caused him.

"Fine," she huffed and thrust the check toward him.

He grabbed the check, stuffed it in his jacket pocket and scribbled his name on the form she'd drawn up. "There. Pleasure doing business with you, Red." Clearly Derek had been spending too much time with Viper. Where once he'd been a desperate gambling addict, now he was simply mean, greedy and spiteful.

She choked back a bitter retort and slid with a jerk out of the booth seat. "Now stay out of my life, Derek. Or I swear I'll call the police and charge you with stalking or extortion or whatever they can make stick."

She spun on her heel to march out of the restaurant, but hadn't made it two steps before he was beside her, shadowing her.

"Zoey, wait." He caught her arm to stop her.

Shaking free of his grip with an angry yank, she snapped, "What?"

"Be careful." The sincerity of his expression shocked her. "Viper...he says he's got plans for you. He says he's not finished with you."

Ice streaked through Zoey's blood. "What does that mean?"

Derek shook his head and jammed his hands in the back pockets of his ripped jeans. "Don't know exactly, but...I thought I should warn you." He backed away a couple of steps, leaving

Zoey staring after him with a cold foreboding coalescing in her chest. "Be careful, Zoey. He's dangerous."

Derek's warning reverberated in Zoey's head as she drove to the hospital to take her shift sitting with Adam. After a brief stop by Holly's room to check on her sister, she settled in the rocking chair next to Matt in PICU. Her brother-in-law held his tiny son like a china doll hooked up to infinite tubes and wires. As he stared at his baby and stroked Adam's fingers, Matt's expression was a poignant combination of fascination, worry and fatherly tenderness.

You said our *baby. That's the first time you ever called it* ours. Gage's voice echoed in her memory, along with the joy that had filled his face…just last night. Before she'd tossed caution to the wind for a few moments of escape and possibly destroyed the best relationship in her life.

She sighed heavily, determined not to give in to the tears that threatened. Matt and Holly needed her to be strong and optimistic. She worked to shelve her own problems and give her family the support they deserved and needed.

"How is he?" she asked, stretching a finger out to caress the small foot closest to her.

Matt glanced up, as if only then noticing she had arrived. "Oh, hi, Zoey." He turned his attention back to Adam, a small grin tugging the corner of his mouth. "My boy's a fighter. Dr. Freeman says he's stable. His vitals all look good. They're going to try to feed him some breast milk later today."

Zoey grinned, relieved to have good news. "I just saw Holly. She's dying to come up here."

Matt nodded. "I bet. She came up for a while earlier today and held him. But her blood pressure has been erratic, so I made her go back to bed to rest."

"Ah, that explains the dictator comment."

Matt looked up, blinking his confusion. "Huh?"

"She said to tell the dictator she was feeling better, and that as soon as the nurse came by to check her vital signs again, no bossy doctor-husband would tell her she couldn't be with her son."

His cheek twitched with amusement, then he settled his gaze on the baby in the crook of his arm again. "Gage stopped by here on his way to the fire station this morning."

At the mere mention of his name, Zoey's pulse stumbled. "Oh?" She dropped her gaze to Adam's tiny mouth and tried to appear nonchalant. "How did he seem?"

"How did he seem?" Matt repeated, sounding puzzled. "Normal. Concerned for us. A little tired maybe, but...aren't we all? I doubt anyone in the family slept more than a couple hours last night." He paused. "Why?"

Zoey jerked her gaze up to Matt's, a nervous patter tripping through her veins. "Uh... no reason." She shrugged and waved him off. Perhaps a little too vigorously.

"Zoey, is something wrong?"

Big mouth. The last thing she'd wanted to do was cause Matt or any of her family more worry. Why didn't she think before she spoke? She gave herself a mental head slap.

"It's nothing…really…" Her throat tightened, and her voice was on the verge of cracking when the PICU nursery door opened and her mother pushed Holly's wheelchair in.

Saved by the bell.

"Well, looks like we've exceeded the visitor limit." Zoey gathered her purse and shoved to her feet. "So I'll head out…"

Matt's curious gaze followed her. No doubt he'd mention her odd question and overzealous denial to Holly, and she'd be questioned later. *Matt said you were acting weird this morning? Is there a problem between you and Gage?*

She hooked her arm in her mother's. "Come on, Mom, we can share an elevator."

Ellen wiggled free. "Not so fast. I want to coo over my grandson for a minute, until the nurses kick me out." Then to Matt, "May I hold him?"

Zoey backed out of the nursery, watching her mother adjust her sterile paper gown and ease the frighteningly small newborn into her arms.

Turning, she headed to the elevator, rode to the ground floor and rushed toward the exit, blinking back tears. Darn her pregnancy hormones for turning her into such a faucet! As she passed the gift shop, she spotted a man in the periphery of her vision.

A tattooed man. With a zigzag buzz cut.

She staggered to a stop and peered past the magazine rack for a better view.

Viper met her stunned gaze and pulled his mouth into a chilling smirk. What was *he* doing *here?*

Zoey didn't hang around to find out. Spinning on her heel, she dashed through the revolving front door and raced across the parking lot.

He says he's got plans for you. Be careful, Zoey. He's dangerous.

A shiver chased down her spine that had nothing to do with the nippy November wind. Once inside her car with the doors locked, she pulled out her cell phone and started to dial Holly's number. To warn her.

But of what? Viper's interest was in her, not her sister. Wasn't it?

Cautioning Holly might only cause her sister undue additional stress when her focus needed to be on her child, not potential dangers of Zoey's imagination.

But forewarned was forearmed.

Not that Matt would let any harm come to his wife or child on his watch. And security around the PICU was pretty tight with security cameras in place.

Stashing her phone again, she cranked the engine and turned up the heat. As she pulled out of the hospital parking lot, she scanned the property. Viper apparently hadn't followed her outside. Why not?

Shuddering and totally creeped out, Zoey hurried home to relieve Rani of babysitting duty. She kept an eye on her rearview mirror, expecting to see a car following her. But none did.

Once home, she hurried inside, a frigid blast of late-fall air chasing her. The thick gray cloud cover did little to dispel her sense of foreboding. Winter had yet to start, and already she missed the sun.

"Aunt Zoey, look!" Pet charged up to her, a calico cat dangling compliantly from her arms.

Zoey frowned. "Where did you get that cat?"

"Guilty," Rani said, coming into the kitchen from the family room. "I'm cat-sitting for a friend while she's away for Thanksgiving—"

"Her name's Eden, and she fetches like a dog!" Pet gushed.

"I thought Pet would get a kick outta playing with her." Rani winced sheepishly. "I hope it's all right. Mr. Gage didn't have a problem with it."

Eden squirmed free of Pet's grasp and jumped to the floor. Pet dropped to her knees to dangle a shoestring that Eden batted, eliciting a giggle from Gage's niece.

Caught completely off guard by the cat's presence and much more concerned with Viper's appearance at the hospital, Zoey fumbled. "I—I guess… Sure. Whatever."

Rani cocked her head to the side. "You okay, Mrs. P.?"

"Yeah, I—" Zoey's thoughts stumbled over the unfamiliar moniker. *Mrs. P.?* Mrs. Powell. Gage's *wife.* "I, uh…" A trembling started deep in her gut.

From now until you decide this marriage…

this arrangement is over, you won't have to worry about me...crossing the line again.

I can't be around you tonight.

Leapin' lizards, she was a wreck. Her screwup with Gage last night. Her concern over Adam. Now Viper was lurking, waiting to strike like a snake coiled in the rocks.

Rani stepped closer and put a comforting hand on Zoey's arm. "Worried about your nephew, huh?"

"I—yeah." Zoey bobbed her head and raked her hair back from her eyes. Jeepers, she had to get ahold of herself. If she hadn't been in such an emotional tailspin last night, she'd have never let things get so far out of hand with Gage, would never have ruined the delicate balance in their friendship.

Instead, she'd hurt Gage, angered him, pushed him away. Now, when she needed him so much to deal with the other disasters in her life, he was more distant than when she'd fled to Europe, when she'd been living in Vegas with Derek.

She was an idiot.

Heaving a heavy sigh, she trudged to the counter and chucked her purse onto it.

"You know, they've really come a long way in preemie care in recent years. More and more, really small babies are surviving and going on to thrive." Rani's voice broke into her fretting. "I'm sure your nephew will be fine."

Zoey flashed Rani the best smile she could muster. "Thanks. I sure hope so."

When her phone sang the refrain of "Tomorrow," she dug for the cellular device in her purse. Held her breath. Prayed it was Gage inviting her to drop by the fire station for lunch.

Right, and maybe the queen will invite her to tea.

But Holly's name and number lit up the screen. Zoey's heart kicked.

Adam!

"What's happened?" she asked without preamble, her voice tight and thin.

"Nothing terrible. Sorry, didn't mean to frighten you."

Zoey released the breath she held and

sank down into a chair at the kitchen table. "Something good, then?"

"Well, a guy came by here looking for you a little while ago. Medium height, funky haircut, piercings. Ring a bell?"

A rock settled in Zoey's chest. "I… What did he…d-do?"

"Nothing. He didn't even give us a name. He just said to let you know a friend of yours from Vegas had been here."

But Viper had seen her at the hospital, knew she'd seen him. If he wanted to talk to her, why hadn't he followed her out to the parking lot, made an attempt to corner her when he'd seen her? What was his game?

Ice filled her veins.

"Zoey?" Holly's voice called her back to the present.

"Um, okay…th-thanks." She wiped nervous perspiration from her palm on her jeans.

"So who is he? How'd he know to look for you here?"

Rani had crouched beside Pet, who was now

scratching Eden behind the ears. The cat was purring and eating up the attention.

Zoey wished her life could be as simple as a cat's. Eat, sleep, play. No mixed messages about who she was and what she was supposed to do with her life. Get all the love she wanted just by being a cat, playing with a string or rubbing against someone's leg.

"He's…no one. Forget him." *If only that were true…* A prick of unease made her add, "If he comes around again, though, be careful. Don't let him get you alone anywhere."

"Why? Is he dangerous?" Concern tightened Holly's tone.

"Probably not." She winced internally at the lie, but she didn't want Holly worrying, possibly aggravating her blood pressure, spurring Matt into confronting the volatile loan shark. "He's…" Zoey fumbled "…more of an annoyance than a danger."

Rani glanced up at the word *danger.* Her eyebrow lifted curiously. After Zoey had disconnected and set her phone aside, the babysitter joined her at the table. "You have someone bothering you, Mrs. P.?"

"Yeah, well…no. I—" Zoey curled her fingers into her palm. "Kinda. Long story. Just don't answer the door for anyone other than me or Gage until further notice. Okay?"

Rani nodded. "Of course."

"Now, if you're okay watching Pet awhile longer, I need a shower and a nap, and then I want to head back to the hospital this afternoon."

Rani flashed an encouraging smile. "I'm at your disposal for as long as you need me."

"Thanks." Zoey pressed a hand to her pregnancy-rounded belly as she headed down the hall to clean up.

As long as she needed Rani? Was the next eighteen years, until her baby left for college, asking too much?

Exhausted and emotionally spent, Gage dragged through the garage door after one of the most grueling nights in all his years with the fire department. If the all-night call to the tire factory on the south side of town hadn't been enough to wear him down, the early-morning house fire in which three members of a small family were killed had done him in. A young girl, who reminded him of Pet in many ways, was now an orphan. Alone in the world. The sight of the young girl in her Dora pajamas, sobbing hysterically and clinging to the family dog, as he and his fellow firefighters had soaked her house had been gut-wrenching. More than one fireman had cried as they drove back to the station. No one had talked. Gage had stared out the window, using every ounce of energy left in him to shove down the emotions clambering inside him.

From an early age, dealing with the constant drama in his family, he'd gotten good at shutting out pain, shutting down his feelings. Protecting himself with a numb detachment.

And then, before he'd left the fire station at the end of his shift, Elaine had called. Frantic. Crying. She'd heard about the tire factory fire and the fireman who'd gone to the hospital with minor injuries. Calming his sister, assuring her he was safe, convincing her not to give up on her rehab or leave the dry-out clinic had been a test of his patience.

All he wanted was to crawl into bed, pull the covers over his head and sleep for the next, oh, two weeks or so.

Zoey was at the kitchen sink, peeling an orange, when he walked into the kitchen from the mudroom. Her eyes met his through her geeky glasses, and she flashed him a tentative grin. "Hey."

He draped his coat over the back of a chair and twitched his cheek in a pathetic excuse for a returned greeting. "Hi."

More than anything he wanted to cross the room to her, pull her into his arms and hug her as if his life depended on it. He needed to feel her close, needed to lose himself in her fruity scent, her warm concern, her soft voice. He needed the murmured encouragements she'd always given him in high school when he ran to her for comfort and a sympathetic ear—not because the words necessarily told him anything that made a difference in his life, but because they meant she was *there* for him.

This morning, though, the wary hesitation in her expression reminded him how unsettled their relationship was. How much stood between them. How badly her rejection from Thanksgiving still stung.

This morning, his best friend was off-limits. He couldn't run to her, couldn't tell her about his perfectly horrid night. He was as alone in the world as the orphaned girl at this morning's fire. At least she had had her dog.

"Have you eaten?" Zoey asked. "I can fix you some breakfast if—"

"No, thanks." Gage blew out a weary sigh. "All I want is a few hours of shut-eye. It's been a long night."

"Oh. I—" She set the orange aside and stepped toward him. "Can we talk first?"

He groaned, shook his head as he started toward the back of the house. "I'd rather not talk about it. I'll be all right."

"Oh. I didn't realize..." she fumbled, wiping her hands on her bathrobe. "I mean...I have...a problem. Something we should talk about. It's… important."

He paused by the entrance to the living room, turned to face her. "Not now, Zoey. I'm really beat. Last night sucked."

Her auburn eyebrows drew together in consternation and surprise. He'd never in his life told her no when she needed something from him. But he was too raw, too worn down, too on edge to deal with any more problems, let alone a Zoey problem, right now.

She fidgeted with the belt of her robe, looking concerned. "What happened? Are you okay?"

Gage pinched the bridge of his nose, battling down a boatload of guilt. "I'm really too tired to talk now. I'll live."

Zoey frowned. "You're sure?"

"Positive." He took a few more steps toward the living room.

"But after your nap, Gage, I need—"

"You need?" he barked, whirling back around to face her stunned expression. Something inside him snapped, his patience buried in the emotional landslide of the past twelve hours. "What about what I need, Zoey?" His voice was several decibels louder than he'd intended, and the hostility in his tone scared him. He heard his father's voice in his, and a chill washed through him.

Zoey gaped at him, unmasked hurt shimmering in her eyes.

Jerking up a hand, palm out, fingers spread, as if he could ward off the waves of disappointment and anguished confusion radiating from her, he backed out of the room. "I can't deal with…any of this…now," he said in a trembling voice barely above a whisper. He swallowed hard, forcing down the taste of bile in his throat. "Not now."

With that, he retreated down the hall in search of privacy, in search of sleep, in search of the strength he needed to shove the last night into the tiny box where he locked his troubled past.

He'd answer for his cold dismissal of Zoey… later.

Over the next few days, Zoey took turns with the rest of her family sitting beside Adam's crib in PICU. Through tedious hours of delicate ministrations and nurturing, baby Adam held his own, improving by microscopic bits that seemed gigantic to the horde of loved ones who held vigil over him. Tiny sips of breast milk. A wet diaper. A mewl of discomfort that indicated strengthening lungs. No event, no matter how small, went uncelebrated.

Despite the good news with Adam, Zoey spent her days looking over her shoulder, expecting to see Viper jump from the shadows at any time. If not for Holly's call about the "friend from Vegas" fitting Viper's description, she could almost convince herself she'd hallucinated Viper that day as she was leaving the hospital. Still, she knew better than to let down her guard. Like his namesake, she had no doubt Viper was lying in wait, ready to strike when she took a careless misstep.

If the tension of watching for Viper's next move weren't enough, the strained silence that had sprung up between herself and Gage since Thanksgiving night broke her heart. When she thought of the way he'd put her off, yelled at her about his needs, turned his back when she'd tried to tell him about Viper and the money Derek had been extorting from her, she wanted to weep. Her feelings had been so bruised by his harsh tone when she'd tried to explain her situation that she hadn't tried again.

Truth was, she *had* relied too heavily on Gage to help her get through the messes she'd made in the past, expected him to still be there when she tested the limits of their friendship. Maybe the best thing she could do for Gage was to handle her mess with Viper and Derek on her own. It was her problem. She'd solve it and not burden Gage with more stress.

One evening early in the week after Adam's birth, Gage drove her home from the hospital, the radio news filling the quiet in the SUV. They were stopped at a red light when he clicked off the report on the stock market and glanced across the front seat to her.

Zoey's pulse kicked up, her hopes soaring that maybe he wanted to talk the way they used to, that maybe they could begin to bridge the uncomfortable rift between them.

Instead he said, "We're out of milk. And Pet has requested canned ravioli for lunch this week. You mind if we stop and grab a few groceries before we go home?"

Not a bridge. Just grocery shopping.

Heart sinking, Zoey forced an agreeable grin past the clawing ache inside. "That's fine."

The supermarket didn't rate high on her scale of best dates, but at least they were doing it together. Between his twenty-four-hour shifts at the fire station and her visiting hours at the hospital, she'd seen precious little of Gage in the past five days. And she missed him.

Not just because his king-size bed felt lonely as heck without him, but also because she had so much she wanted to tell him, share with him. The way she used to in high school.

The day's events in the PICU. The progress of her own pregnancy. Pet's return to school from Thanksgiving break.

She wanted to talk to him the way she saw her sisters casually chat with their husbands about anything and everything. Sharing a smile or a nagging thought. A comment about a TV program. A loving word of comfort and encouragement.

If she'd had any sign things were back to normal between her and Gage, she'd even try again to confess her predicament with Derek and Viper.

But Gage had lapsed into the role of a polite stranger. He was stiff and formal around her. Considerate but distant. Detached.

Gage pulled in a parking space at the grocery store and cut the engine. A memory from high school, when they'd come together to this same store to buy snacks for a late-night study session, flickered through Zoey's mind with a melancholy tug on her heart. As he turned to slide out the driver's door, she caught Gage's arm. "Hey, remember our senior year when we came here before Mr. Mansfield's chemistry exam?"

"Yeah, I remember. We made ourselves sick on junk food that night." He dropped his gaze to her hand, resting on his arm, and he shrugged away from her touch.

Another pluck of disappointment weighted her chest as he pulled back, but she tried to keep her tone light. "Wanna play the game we did that night? We have five minutes to see who can find the weirdest thing for sale in the store."

He sighed and shook his head as he climbed out of the front seat. "Not tonight. I'm tired, and we gotta get home and relieve Rani of monster duty."

"Oh. Right." A lump swelled in Zoey's throat, and she swallowed hard as she stepped out of the SUV, forcing the knot back down. She didn't so much care about the silly game as she did the lost camaraderie with Gage.

Even though he waited to walk inside with her, he didn't make any of the familiar gestures to which she'd grown accustomed since high school. An arm around her shoulders. A solicitous hand at the base of her back. Quiet signals that said, "I'm here with you, here for you."

Inside the store, while she snagged them a cart, Gage took a basket from the stack by the door. "I'll get the milk and ravioli. You pick out anything you want, and I'll meet you at the checkout."

Zoey blinked at him, hurt. He didn't even

want to *shop* together? Maybe he was just trying to save time, be efficient. But she felt rejected, pushed away. Was he punishing her for refusing to sleep with him? Didn't he understand she was trying to protect their friendship?

Bang-up job of that you've done. He's more distant than ever now.

"I guess I—"

But he'd already cut through the produce area toward the back of the store where the dairy items were displayed.

Frowning her displeasure, Zoey shoved the cart toward the snack aisle. Suddenly she was in the mood to drown her sorrows in a box of chocolate cupcakes. She'd have to hide the treats from Pet—assuming there were any left when she got done with them tonight—because a sugary treat like cupcakes made the monster bounce off the walls.

Her stomach rumbled and tumbled a bit as she tossed a large box of frosted mini-cakes in the cart. Maybe, for the baby's sake, she should buy something healthy to eat, as well. Casting a longing gaze down the main store aisle in

search of Gage—he wasn't anywhere in sight—
she rolled the cart to the aisle with the display
of canned fruits. A jar of applesauce caught
her eye. Applesauce was healthy, right? She
studied the selection, boggled by the choices.
Sweetened. Unsweetened. Chunky. Cherry-
flavored. Light. Original recipe.

She sensed more than saw someone move up
behind her. Close behind her. So close it could
only be Gage. Unspoken societal rules wouldn't
have allowed a stranger to move so close. She
smelled the familiar scent of his soap, and her
heart fluttered. She stood motionless, afraid to
move and scare him away. She wanted to savor
his nearness, the hope that maybe he was tearing down the wall he'd erected between them
these past several days.

He shifted, and his chest skimmed her back.

But something wasn't right.

She caught the scent of cigarettes clouding the
crisp soap scent. The chest was at the wrong
height. Wrong clothing. A chill crawled down
her spine.

Just as she turned to see who was there, an

arm reached around her for a can on the shelf. An arm with a snake tattoo.

"I love pineapple. Don't you?" Viper asked. "It's so sweet. Juicy." The lascivious glint in his eyes made the words sound crude.

Zoey gasped and stumbled backward, flinching away from him and knocking a display of instant oatmeal to the floor. "Wh-what do you want? Why are you following me?"

His lips curled in a satisfied grin. "I'm just shopping for pineapple, Red."

"Stay away from me! And stay away from my family!" She aimed a trembling finger at him and struggled for a breath. "I'm warning you, if you don't—"

The humor fled Viper's face in an instant, and he grabbed her wrist, jerking her close.

Her heart jumped to her throat, and her pulse thundered in her ears.

"I make the demands here, Red. Not you," he hissed in her ear. His hot breath slithered along her neck and made her skin crawl. "Just do as I say, and no one gets hurt. Got it?"

As quickly as he'd grabbed her, he pushed her

away. He cut a look to the older woman who pushed her cart past them and flashed an oily smile. "Evening, ma'am."

Zoey's knees shook, and she braced her weight against the shopping cart to keep from slumping to the floor.

Where was Gage? She had to find him, had to get away from Viper...

But as stealthily as he'd appeared, Viper turned and disappeared down the aisle. His parting shot still clanging in her head.

Do as I say, and no one gets hurt.

He hadn't made any demands yet, but the threat he posed was clear enough. And her duty to protect her family remained utmost in her mind. She had to do everything she could to make sure her family didn't suffer because of her mistakes.

Zoey seemed unusually agitated as they checked out and headed outside to the SUV. Her gaze darted around the dark parking lot, her eyes bright with distress. Her bottom lip swelled from the abuse of her teeth, and she hugged herself against the bite of the November air.

Instinctively, he started to pull her into a one-armed embrace to help her ward off the cold wind, but a lightning flash of memory struck his heart, sending concentric ripples of pain through him in its wake. He quickly tucked his hand into his jeans pocket and squelched the urge to comfort her. *Keep it platonic. She doesn't want you.*

Guilt kicked Gage in the ribs. He'd seen the hurt in her eyes when he'd pulled away from her touch earlier, but avoiding her was a matter of self-preservation. The memory of their aborted lovemaking was still too fresh, too raw, too vivid in his mind. The silky softness of her skin, the sweetness of her kiss, the mind-blowing eroticism of her caress when she'd stroked his—

Gage gritted his teeth and shoved the thought aside before it fully formed. How the hell was he going to survive the next few months without imploding from sexual frustration? Just a simple touch, like when she'd stopped him from climbing out of the car, sent shock waves through him.

Wasn't it bad enough that her rejection left his heart feeling as if it had gone twelve rounds with Evander Holyfield? At least his father's abuse had taught him to wall off his emotions enough to survive life's disappointments.

But he'd never learned how to shut off his attraction to his best friend, and now, with the taste of her lips still so fresh in his memory, he was slowly going insane. Only by keeping her at arm's length could he hold the pain, the unrequited desire at bay.

As they loaded the few bags of groceries into the SVU, the slam of a car door near them made Zoey jump, and concern overrode his caution. "Are you all right, Zee? You're acting all nervous and flipped out."

She jerked a startled look to him. "No! I mean, yes...I'm fine," she said quickly. Too quickly.

Maybe the stress of her nephew being in PICU was eating at her. Or maybe the strain in their friendship was wearing on her the way it was him. He should ask her about it. If he were a good friend, a good husband, he'd press her to open up, tell him what was bothering her. Before last Thursday night, he would have. But frankly the idea of having a talk that intimate, that emotional, that honest left him in a cold sweat. He couldn't come that close to her pain without brushing up against his own misery.

So he let her nervous behavior, her worried eyes, her too-quick answer slide.

And felt like a heel for it.

Climbing onto the driver's seat, Gage scrubbed a hand over his face and sighed. He couldn't live like this, walking a tightrope, tiptoeing the fine line between the platonic relationship she wanted and the intimate, open, sexual *marriage* he craved.

Halfway didn't cut it. Halfway chewed up his guts and scraped his nerve endings. Halfway hurt like hell.

Maybe they'd both be better off if they ended this charade of a marriage and went their separate ways now instead of waiting for the baby to come. Maybe a divorce was the only way to save what was left of their tattered friendship.

Gage squeezed the steering wheel and sent Zoey a covert glance. The moonlight danced over her ivory cheeks and highlighted the fiery streaks in her hair. His heart fisted.

She was so beautiful. So out of reach. So forbidden.

Like she had always been for this punk from the wrong side of the tracks.

Some days he really hated being Zoey Bancroft's friend.

Chapter 11

The next afternoon, Zoey was running late getting to Pet's school to pick her up. The carpool line had already dwindled to only two other delayed moms and the school yard was empty, except for the duty teacher, Pet...and a man smoking a cigarette as he yukked it up with the duty teacher.

Zoey's pulse slammed into overdrive. Damn Viper! What was he doing here?

Ice filled her veins.

Same thing he'd been doing at the store last night. Intimidating her.

She squealed to a stop, jammed the SUV into Park and hurried out of the front seat. "Pet!"

Gage's niece, who'd had her head down as she dug in the dirt with a stick, looked up when Zoey called. Viper ruffled Pet's hair as the girl grabbed her backpack and skipped toward Zoey as if she hadn't a care in the world. As if a crazy, violent loan shark wasn't circling in the water. Daring to touch her. Taunting Zoey with his proximity to Pet.

Zoey's breath hung in her lungs until Pet reached the SUV, oblivious to the danger Viper posed.

That's good. Pet's life should be carefree, safe.

Zoey took a deep breath trying to calm the tremble that raced through her and hide her own fear from Pet.

While Pet clambered into the backseat and held her arms out of the way for Zoey to buckle the booster seat, Zoey slanted a look toward Viper. As expected, he was watching her, and he sent her a nerve-rattling smirk.

"Your friend is funny," Pet said, giggling and leaning forward to look out the door at Viper.

Fresh waves of cold terror rushed through Zoey. "My friend?"

"That guy." Pet pointed, then returned a wave when Viper wiggled his fingers at her. "He has a funny haircut and told me silly jokes."

"He's not my friend," she returned automatically and regretted her abruptness when Pet frowned. "N-not really."

Zoey's hands shook as she fumbled to buckle Pet into her seat as fast as possible. She had to get them out of there. Now. Before Viper decided to approach them. Before he made his next move.

"He said he was. He knew my name and your name and Uncle Gage, and he told me and Ms. Collins about an elephant who wore pajamas…" Pet jabbered.

Zoey's mouth dried when the duty teacher stepped away from Viper and headed inside. What had he told the woman? Why hadn't the teacher recognized him as a threat?

The booster-seat buckle clicked into place,

and Zoey whipped the back door closed and ran back to the driver's side.

She'd have to call the school first thing tomorrow and warn them about Viper. She'd have to explain to the school—

Zoey stopped, tears pricking her eyes, blurring her vision as she stared through the windshield at the man now lighting a cigarette as he propped a hip against the bicycle rack.

Viper was at Pet's school. He'd talked to her. He'd touched her head.

The sensation of spiders under her skin crawled through Zoey. She was out of time. She couldn't pretend this problem would go away. She couldn't lull herself into believing she could handle the situation alone by appeasing Derek or Viper with payoffs. She had to tell someone what was going on. The police. Her parents. *Gage.*

Once again, her foolish good intentions, her reckless bad decisions had brought trouble to her loved ones' front steps. Disgust and self-loathing churned in her gut.

She drove away from the school, shaking head

to toe, sick with dread, regret, guilt. Once the school was gone from her rearview mirror, she pulled into the driveway of a white ranch-style home and dug out her cell phone.

"Why are we stopping here?" Pet asked. "This isn't our house."

"I know, honey. I have to make a call. I—"

Gage answered his phone on the second ring. "Zoey? Everything all right?"

That he'd assume her call meant something was wrong spoke for how little they talked about good things, mundane things, *anything* anymore. That he was right about there being trouble, trouble that was her fault, drove another nail of bitter remorse into her heart.

"Something's happened, Gage. I...did something that...well, I can see now it was a mistake. I had the best intentions, but—"

"What's happened?"

His what-now? tone scraped her guilty conscience.

She lifted her gaze to Pet's reflection in the rearview mirror. "I can't talk about it now. Little ears are listening. But tonight—"

"I'll be home tomorrow morning around eight-thirty. Will it keep until then?"

She pressed a hand to her mouth, forcing herself to breathe slowly through her nose, regaining control. Just talking to Gage, hearing his voice made her feel somewhat better.

"Yeah. Tomorrow morning is fine." Maybe by then she'd have figured a way out of this mess. Or at least figured out a way to tell Gage what a royal pickle she'd gotten herself, her family, in.

"Whatever it is, try not to worry, okay? The stress isn't good for the baby." His voice dipped to a low, comforting timbre she'd heard so many times over the years—so safe and familiar, tears of longing prickled her eyes. "We'll figure something out. Everything will be okay."

She'd give anything if she could be sure that were true. "Okay."

"By the way, I got your...gift. But...am I supposed to know what the pineapple is all about?"

Zoey blinked, not certain she'd heard him right. "What?"

"The can of pineapple you put in my locker

here at the station. The note says, 'With love from Red.'"

It's so sweet. Juicy.

Fear landed another sucker punch in her gut. Viper was nothing if not thorough. He'd made clear she knew he could get to anyone in her family—her sister at the hospital, Pet at school, Gage at work—whenever he wanted. If she didn't meet his demands. If she defied him and went to the police.

"You hate being called Red. Why would you sign it Red?" Gage's voice pulled her out of the nightmare turn of her thoughts. "And am I missing some symbolism here with the pineapple? Some private joke I've forgotten?"

"I didn't send it. I didn't write the note. Oh, God...Gage, be careful. It's a warning. From a dangerous guy who's...got me in a difficult position."

"Aunt Zoey, can we go now?" Pet whined, impatience and pleading rife in her tone. "I gotta pee!"

"I— Okay, Pet. Just...hold it a little longer."

She shifted into Reverse and backed out onto the road again. "I gotta go, Gage."

"Wait, Zoey," Gage growled, his voice now darkly concerned. "What the hell's going on? You've been acting skittish and upset for days now. I wrote it off as worry over Adam. Now you tell me someone dangerous is after you—" He huffed a harsh sigh. "That's it. Forget morning. I'm coming home now."

"No, Gage. You don't have to—" But even as she tried to dissuade him, she prayed he would come. She needed his reassurance, needed his strength—needed *him*.

"I'll tell the chief we've had a family emergency. If someone has threatened you, or if you think you and Pet could be in danger, there's no way I'm staying here tonight, leaving you alone at the house."

Zoey pulled up to a four-way stop, relieved to see no other cars at the intersection. She stayed where she was until she finished her call, reluctant to talk on her cell and drive at the same time. She had enough distractions in her life, enough problems to deal with without asking for a car accident.

"I'm so sorry, Gage. It seems like I've been nothing but a headache to you since you arrived in Las Vegas. Heck, I've been a pain in your a—" she caught herself and flicked a glance at Pet's rearview mirror image "—um, neck...for years now."

"Stop it, Zee," Gage warned. "We'll talk when I get home. Lock the doors when you get inside. Okay?"

As if he had to remind her. She'd been locking doors and looking behind her for weeks now. She was ready for this mess with Viper to be resolved.

She could only hope it didn't cost her what was left of her friendship to Gage in the process.

Gage's gut knotted tighter with dread the closer he got to his house. He had no idea what sort of danger Zoey might be in. Could it be related to Derek and the thugs who'd been after her in Las Vegas? The memory of her bruised face when he'd found her at the emergency shelter in Vegas lit a flash fire in his blood. Just how much trouble was she in? How far out of hand had things gotten?

And how was he supposed to protect himself, keep an emotional distance from her if she needed his help unsnaring herself from a real problem? Even though he'd defend her with his dying breath if he had to, he preferred taking a physical beating, like the ones his dad doled out, than facing the pain of any deeper, unrequited emotional entanglement with Zoey. A guy's heart could only take so much abuse.

He pulled his truck into the driveway, holding his breath, not sure what form of disaster might be waiting when he walked inside.

"Zoey!" he called as he shed his coat, tossing it over the back of the sofa and prowled deeper into the house, looking for signs of life.

"Noooo!" he heard Pet whine. "I don't like that video anymore. I wanna play with Uncle Gage!"

"No more fussing, Pet. I need time to talk to Gage, and then he has to go back to work.

If you'll stay in here and watch TV for a little while, I'll play with you after dinner."

He followed the sound of voices to the master bedroom where Zoey was trying valiantly to settle Pet into a *Dora the Explorer* DVD.

"I don't like Dora anymore!" Pet screamed and threw the DVD case across the room.

Gage tensed, ready to step in and battle the five-year-old, when Zoey straightened her spine and aimed a finger at the far corner of the room.

"Time-out. Throwing things and yelling are not good behavior," Zoey said, her voice calm but firm.

Gage eased back into the hall, out of sight, and observed. Intrigued.

Pet glared at Zoey obstinately. "No!"

Zoey motioned to the corner again, repeating her directions. Then, when Pet still refused to comply, she lifted the wiggly protesting girl and set her in the corner. Squatting in front of her, Zoey said, "I really need your cooperation right now, Pet. Gage and I have to talk without interruption. Can you please help me out by watching the TV or working on a puzzle or some other quiet game for a little while?"

"But I want to play with Gage." Pet crossed her arms over her chest and poked out her bottom lip.

"I'm sure he'd be happy to play with you another time. Right now, I need you to be a big girl, no whining, and do something quiet back here until dinnertime." Zoey stroked Pet's cheek with a loving hand. "If you'll do this for me, then I'll play Chutes and Ladders with you before bed."

Pet scowled, considering the offer. "Okay. But I don't want Dora."

"Fine. No Dora. You pick the DVD. But throwing things isn't the way to get what you want, is it?"

Pet shook her head, her expression contrite.

I'll be damned. Gage grinned to himself and stepped farther back into the hall while Zoey set the time-out egg timer and left Pet in the corner to think about her behavior.

When Zoey emerged into the hall, she gasped,

startled. "Gage, jeez!" She clasped a hand over her heart. "I didn't hear you come in."

"Sorry, didn't mean to scare you." He hitched a head toward the bedroom as they moved down the hall to the living room. "Good job in there. You've come a long way from throwing mimicking tantrums to get her attention."

Zoey's cheek twitched in a weak grin. "I've been reading a lot of parenting books. I'm gonna have to know this stuff when the baby comes, and I want to do the right thing with Pet and..." Her eyes filled with tears, and she wrapped her arms around herself as if chilled. "Oh, Gage...I'm so scared."

He took a step toward her to comfort her before he caught himself, backed off. Old habits die hard. "What's going on, Zee?"

She lowered herself onto the couch, and he sat at the opposite end, waiting for her to explain herself. He struggled not to think about the last time they'd both been on that couch. Just six days ago...

"I thought I was protecting you and Pet...my parents...I never thought it would go this far."

Her voice cracked. "I thought if I did what they asked, they'd be happy and go away. I—"

"Who would go away? Zoey, what did you do?"

"Derek followed me here. After we left Vegas."

The other man's name landed in Gage's gut like an anvil. Ancient jealousy and unease flared in his blood.

Zoey stared down at her fidgeting hands and bit her bottom lip. "He asked for money. He said he needed my help paying off his debt to this loan shark named Viper."

Gage groaned and rubbed his face, seeing where this was going. "Please tell me you didn't give him more money than he already stole from you in Vegas."

She hesitated. "I— He made threats...veiled threats about Pet and my parents and...you."

"Zee..." Gage flopped back on the sofa cushions and covered his eyes with his arm. "How much?"

"A thousand the first time."

He jerked his arm from his face and narrowed

a stunned look on her. "The *first* time? You gave him money more than once?"

She flinched at his sharp tone, and he struggled to rein in his temper before she spoke again. "At the time, I thought it was the best thing to do. When I told him no, he..."

A tear spilled onto her cheek, and his heart lurched. She swiped at it as she continued, her voice trembling. "He threatened to sue for custody of my baby."

Gage's chest filled with lead twice over. First, hearing her revert to "my baby," and second, learning Derek had made a threatening claim of any kind on Zoey's child.

"He said how he'd hate to see anything bad happen to Pet or you..." Zoey sniffed and sent him a look that pleaded for understanding. For forgiveness. "I was so scared he'd do something to hurt one of you. That he'd try to take my baby, purely out of spite."

His mind reeled, trying to comprehend the scope of her predicament, why she'd made the bad choices she had. "Why didn't you tell me any of this before now?"

"I tried to. Tuesday morning when you came home from the fire station, but—"

"I bit your head off." Compunction sucker punched him, and he scrubbed a hand over his face, groaning.

She rubbed a hand over the rounded swell of her stomach and nodded. "I know giving in to Derek's demands was like the U.S. negotiating with terrorists. But I was scared. I thought I could protect you and my family from him if I—"

"Why didn't you call the police?" he interrupted, his jaw tight.

Her shoulders sagged. "At first, because I thought giving him the thousand would make him go away. A thousand dollars didn't seem like a bad price for my family's safety and peace of mind."

When he pulled a face in disbelief, she lifted her trembling chin and swiped another tear from her cheek with an aggravated flick of her finger. "I know. I know!" She huffed her frustration with herself. "Later, when Derek threatened to sue for custody—"

Her voice cracked, and he steeled himself against the answering tug in his heart. Despite her good intentions, she'd deceived him, used his hard-earned money to pay off her ex, chummed the water for a Vegas loan shark. Heat prickled his neck as his temper rose, his patience with her waning.

"That's what you used the thousand from my account for." A statement, not a question.

"I'll pay you back. I've told you all along, I'll pay you back."

"That's not the point."

She cleared her throat before continuing. "I w-was afraid of defying him, afraid he really would try to take my baby away and…"

Gage's chest tightened, imagining Zee's scumbag ex taking her baby, the baby Gage still wanted to claim as his own.

"When I remembered how Viper reacted to my threat to call the police when he came looking for Derek in Las Vegas—" She touched her eye, reminding him of the bruise that had marred her face when he'd found her at the emergency shelter, and his blood pressure spiked higher. "I was sure the easiest thing to do, the best way to protect my family and you was not to provoke Viper. Things actually quieted down for a while, Derek left me alone for weeks. I thought everything was over, but then—" She squeezed her eyes shut and bit her bottom lip.

Gage gritted his back teeth, stared at his shoes. "Never mind. I can guess."

"Viper hasn't made any specific demands yet but…he's laying the groundwork. Intimidating me. He was at Pet's school today."

Gage jerked his head up, his pulse tripping.

"And he was at the grocery store the other night. And the hospital. He put the pineapple in your locker at work. His way of telling me he knows how to get to the people I love," she said morosely.

Gage shoved to his feet. He'd heard enough. No one threatened his family and got away with it.

Tension flowed through him like electricity sparking from a live wire. He flexed and balled his hands, needing an outlet for his fury. "Where is this Viper now?"

"I don't know. He—" She glanced up at him, surveyed his rigid, combative stance, and her face paled. "Gage, no!" she rasped and struggled to her feet. "This is exactly why I didn't tell you sooner! He's dangerous."

He balled his fists and rolled his shoulders. "I can handle him."

"No! You can't confront him! I won't let you put yourself in harm's way for—"

"Zoey, you can't let a bully push you around. Living with my dad taught me that. If you give in, you seal your fate as his perennial victim." He flashed on the night he'd finally stood up to his old man, defended himself. He'd been devastated, sick with guilt and shame, for having returned his father's blows on graduation night, but his father had never hit him again. Elaine and his mother hadn't been as lucky.

"Brawling with him isn't the answer."

He tasted an ancient bitterness at the back of his throat, the bile of protective anger. No way in hell would he let anyone hurt him or his family again. "Maybe not. But this punk threatening you has to know he can't get away with—"

Zoey gasped and clutched her belly.

Fury morphed in an instant to concern. Holly had gasped and doubled over just like that when she went into premature labor. Gage's breath stuck in his lungs as icy fingers of fear crawled through him. "What? What's wrong?"

If something happened to Zee's baby…

She winced again and slowly sat back down on the couch, rubbing a hand over her stomach. "The baby's got his foot in my ribs. He's really started kicking hard lately."

"Is that normal?" Gage eased down beside her, rubbing his sweaty hands on the legs of his work pants. "Are you okay?"

Zee lifted red-rimmed eyes to his, and her cheek twitched in a sad grin. "The baby's okay. Don't worry."

He exhaled the knot of tension clogging his throat, buried his face in his hands and rubbed his eyes with his palms. The emotions he usually kept a tight rein on now coursed freely through him, twisting him up, confusing him.

The adrenaline of remnant anger, the instantaneous jolt of fear when he thought of Zoey losing the baby, the gut-deep quake of frustration with Zoey's bad decisions. *Get a grip, Powell. You're no good to her if you fall apart.*

"Wanna feel?" Zoey's voice was so soft, the question so tentative, he thought for a moment that the query had been a trick of his imagination.

He turned a dubious gaze toward her. "Hmm?"

"Do you want to feel the baby move?" she asked. "He's really squirming right now."

His attention darted to her pregnancy bump, his heart giving a lurch.

Did he want to feel the baby move? Hell, yeah.

But the idea terrified him, too. How could he share such a tender, intimate moment with Zoey, feel the warmth of her body as he laid his hands on the place where she grew a new life, and not fall in love with her all over again? How could he handle the pain of bonding with a tiny being who might never be a part of his life? He swallowed hard.

He couldn't. His feelings were too raw right now.

He needed to keep his distance, needed to—

She reached for his wrist and pulled his hand toward her belly.

Gage tensed, pulled back as if burned. "Zoey, no. I don't think—"

She ignored his protest and grabbed his wrist again, flattened his palm against her baby with her own hand. "Feel that lump? That's his foot."

He held his breath. Avoided her eyes. Gave her a jerky nod.

With a gentle tug, he tried to extract his hand from hers before—

The lump under his hand twitched, rolled. Kicked.

Gage sucked in a sharp breath, and Zoey chuckled.

"Yeah, try sleeping with that action pounding your bladder."

He couldn't help it. He raised his eyes to meet hers.

And was snared in the tangled web of emotions staring back at him. Wistful joy and expectation glowed in her jade eyes and held him spellbound. Dark fear and regret creased her brow and pulled at her lips. Fragile hope and wonder tinted her freckled cheeks. An errant corkscrew of auburn hair fell across her forehead, as unruly and arbitrary as the woman herself.

Bittersweet longing slashed through him, and he clenched his teeth, fighting the burning sensation in his sinuses, the knotting in his throat. He felt himself sinking, drowning.

Save yourself.

But he couldn't. He'd never been able to extract himself from the gravitational pull of Zoey Bancroft. Instead he placed his other hand beside his first, cupping her rounded belly between his palms. His heart tapped an expectant rhythm as they waited, his gaze locked with hers.

Another flutter and bump under his hands

stirred a breath-stealing awe in his chest for the miracle of the new life growing inside her. A hesitant smile touched her lips. And jabbed another blade of double-edged yearning in his soul. He wanted this. Wanted Zoey. So much. Impulsive recklessness and all. He always had. Even when a future with her had been a pipe dream.

Do you really think you're anything 'cept a pity case for that girl? Don't kid yourself, boy. Her kind don't want trailer trash for anything permanent.

But if his father could see them now, what would he say? Did it matter that Gage had clawed his way out of the hellish circumstances of his youth and made a life for himself? Zoey still didn't see him any differently. Nothing had changed.

As she held his gaze, the spark of maternal wonder in Zoey's expression melted to heart-breaking sadness. Moisture puddled in her eyes, and his pulse shifted into overdrive.

What had she seen in his face that altered her mood so abruptly? Gage struggled to school his face, shove down the painful track of his thoughts, but her gaze still held his transfixed.

"Please forgive me," she whispered, her fingers curling around the hands he pressed to her stomach. "I've done nothing but mess up your life, hurt you, drag you down with my screwups for years. Anyone else would have walked away, given up on me a long ago. I don't know why you stay, but I—"

"I'm hungry," Pet whined as she stomped into the living room and flopped onto the other end of the couch.

The spell was broken like the bursting of a bubble. Pop.

Breaking the stare that had mesmerized him, Gage snatched his hands from Zoey's, from the squirming kicks of her baby, and rocked back against the sofa cushions.

"How much longer do you have to talk grown-up talk?"

He drew a deep breath to clear his head and dragged his hands over his mouth, his chin. "We're done."

"Finally!" Pet said with dramatic exasperation.

"We are?" Zoey frowned. "But I—"

"Go wash your hands and set the table, Squirt."

As Pet scampered off to do as told, Gage shoved to his feet, steeled himself before facing his wife. "Zoey, you know what has to be done. You've known all along, but you fought your better judgment because you were afraid."

He hazarded a glance at Zoey. Her eyes were wide, her face pale. "For my family. For you. For the baby. Afraid that Viper would hurt you. Afraid that Derek would try to take—"

"No."

Zoey barked a laugh that lacked humor. "What do you mean no?"

"Come on, Zee. That's not what you really feared most."

"Wh— I—" She gaped at him, a look of incredulous dismay.

He held up a hand to forestall her arguments. "I'm not saying it wasn't part of it, that they weren't legitimate concerns. But—" He paused, glanced away gathering his courage. What Zoey needed was brutal honesty. But the truth would hurt her, and he hated being the one to cause her any pain. He'd spent the past eleven years trying to protect her, trying to spare her pain.

So maybe he was partly to blame, for letting her continue to live the lie she'd been living.

"But what, Gage?" she asked, a note of defensiveness tingeing her voice.

He took a deep breath and dived into the murky waters he'd avoided until now. "If you were honest with yourself, you'd know you were scared most for yourself."

His gut tightened, seeing the shadow that crept over her face, but he plowed on. If she hated him for telling her the truth, then so be it. Their relationship had already gotten hopelessly tangled, permanently cracked, perhaps fatally wounded.

"You were scared of admitting to me, to your family that you'd messed up. Scared of showing the people around you that you'd failed. You try to cover one screwup by making another bad decision until it snowballs out of control. You try to handle things on your own rather than admit to the people who love you that you've made a mistake. Well, news flash, Zee. We already know your tendency for screwups. We know that you run from problems rather than face hard choices."

She struggled to her feet, defiance flashing in her eyes. "I don't—"

"You do! You stormed out of your parents' house two years ago after fighting with your father—" he made a sweeping gesture with his hand, emphasizing his point "—and spent two years with a loser who was stealing from you rather than admit to yourself or your family that you'd been wrong about Derek."

Her gaze darted away. The wrinkle in her brow and tightening of her mouth told him he'd struck a nerve.

"And you ran from me after graduation night rather than face the 'worst blunder of your life.'" A sharp ache stabbed his chest as he threw her words back at her. "You could have talked to me about it, told me you didn't want our relationship to go that direction, but you didn't even give me a goodbye. No, facing me the morning after, facing your mistake would have been too hard, too awkward, too painful. So you ran."

A sob hiccuped from her throat. "I've said I was sorry."

He scoffed and shook his head. "Yeah. Big deal. My father said he was sorry for beating his family, but it didn't stop him from doing it again."

Zoey gasped, pain etched in her wan complexion.

"Your sorry is worthless, Zoey. You're always sorry, but you never *change.*"

She seemed to shrink before him, drawing into herself, closing down, shutting him out. He'd lanced a festering wound, but now he couldn't stop the poison that spewed from the years-old injuries he'd kept buried for so long.

"If you're really sorry, then do something about it! Stop lying to yourself. Admit when you are wrong and *deal with it* instead of hiding or running or covering it up with more stupid mistakes." He was shaking. From the inside out, he quaked with a terror that he'd hurt Zoey beyond repair. Tears spilled down her cheeks, and she refused to look at him.

He felt awful. Gut sick. As if he'd kicked a puppy. Or told a preschool class there was no Santa Claus.

Or berated an insecure pregnant woman.

And lost his best friend.

He drew an unsteady breath and released it as a hiss through clenched teeth. "Zee, the thing is—"

"I get it, okay?" She spun away and stalked toward the back of the house. Running. Again. "I'm a screwup, and everyone knows it. Message received."

"Wait. I—"

But she didn't stick around to hear any more of his harsh assessment. The bedroom door slammed, and he dropped onto the sofa with a sigh.

Brilliant, Powell. You handled that so well.

"The thing is—" he muttered to the empty room "—we all love you anyway. And that will never change. The one you're really hurting with your bad decisions is yourself."

* * *

Zoey thought she might throw up. She sat on the edge of the bathtub and fought for a breath. The weight of Gage's angry words sat on her lungs like a boulder and gnawed at her gut with razor-sharp teeth. She'd thought his distance and silence had been painful, but hearing the man she trusted and cared for most in the world tell her she was a gutless screwup and a stupid, lying coward who was in denial hurt more than she could imagine.

Because he was right. On most counts.

But he was only half right about her darkest fear. The thing she feared most was that the people she loved would see the real her, the Zoey she'd been trying to hide, Zoey the screwup…and wouldn't love her anymore. They'd see the ugly truth of her messed-up, restless, confused self and throw their hands up in frustration. They'd give up on her and walk away.

As Gage's verbal barrage rang in her ears, all her childhood insecurities of not measuring up to her sisters, not having the discipline or direction her parents could point to with pride rushed back. A dark sense of futility settled over her like a murky fog.

For years, she'd fought her nature, tried to suppress her impulsiveness, her restlessness, her tendency for drama. As she'd learned to do on stage, she'd pretended to be someone she wasn't, wanting the applause, the approval, the acceptance that she couldn't get by being herself. But the real Zoey wouldn't be tamed. Trying to be someone she wasn't left a vast emptiness inside her. She'd searched Europe for that elusive something that would make her truly happy, and she'd thought she'd found it in Derek. Someone to love her for who she was, someone to build a life with, someone…like Gage.

But now, because of her propensity for trouble, her knack for impulsive, bad decisions—despite her best intentions—her worst fears were reality. Gage had seen her at her worst. Had seen the true depths of her hopelessness and called her to task for her true nature.

The friend she'd always relied on to be there had reached his limit. The man who'd never raised his voice with her had run out of patience. The one person she needed most to love her unconditionally had seen her true nature and thrown in the towel.

She raised her gaze and met her reflection in the mirror over the sink.

You're always sorry, but you never change.

Gage was wrong about that, too. She had changed in the past few weeks. She'd seen with staggering clarity what *really* mattered to her—her family.

Not independence. Not adventure. Not some false idea of freedom.

Adam's premature birth had taught her the fragility of life. Seeing her family's willingness to welcome her back into the fold, compared to Derek's selfish abuse of her affections, showed her the depth of her family's bond. Her father's forgiveness, despite her short temper and stubborn inability to admit her mistakes, demonstrated the power of parental love she would pass on to her baby.

Zoey leaned toward the mirror image, staring deep into the green eyes her father had given each of his daughters. Bancroft eyes, her mother called them. With a twinge in her heart, Zoey wished green eyes weren't the only Bancroft trait she'd inherited. If she had more of her father's confidence, practicality and discerning—

Life is ten percent what happens to you and ninety percent how you respond to what happens, she heard her father saying the day she and Gage had returned from Las Vegas.

How you respond...

You know what has to be done...but you fought your better judgment because you were afraid.

Zoey straightened her back, squared her shoulders and swiped her cheeks dry with her sleeve. She'd show Gage she could change. She could face her fear and do the right thing. She could admit she'd been wrong and deal with it the way she should have from the beginning instead of trying to hide her screwup from her best friend and her family.

Hoisting herself from the side of the bathtub,

she waddled determinedly into the bedroom to the phone beside the bed.

And called the police.

Chapter 12

"So what did the police say?" Ellen Bancroft asked her daughter the next morning.

With a bittersweet tug in her heart, Zoey stared through the plate-glass window, watching Gage play catch with Miles and Pet in her parents' backyard. The tension between her and Gage this morning had been as taut as a piano wire, the silence, deafening, the growing distance between them, heartbreaking.

"They said there wasn't much they could do." Explaining the whole ugly scenario with Derek's extortion and Viper's menace to her parents had been draining, humiliating. Unavoidable. "Viper hasn't actually done anything illegal. There is no law against him stopping by a school yard at the end of the day or going to the grocery store when I'm there. I don't know where he's staying or what his real name is. I have next to nothing except suspicions and implications.

"With Derek, I can't *prove* he used intimidation or coercion when he demanded money. It would be my word against his. I have nothing in writing, no tape recordings of his threats, no witnesses. What I do have is a history with him that shows we pooled our assets, such as they were, for months. It looks like I was just continuing to give money of my free will to a man I had a relationship with. Period. Without proof of extortion, I have no case."

"What about when Derek kidnapped Pet? That's sure as hell illegal!" her father said, squeezing the armrests of his overstuffed chair with a white-knuckle grip.

"He didn't kidnap her so much as encourage her to hide from me. He never touched her. Never held her against her will. She sneaked away from me, and he convinced her to play hide-and-seek with him." Her inattention that day still twisted her up with guilt.

"What does Gage say about all this?" her mother asked, waving a hand toward the window. Outside, Gage had Pet on his back and Miles tackling his leg as he lumbered across the yard, dragging both kids toward an invisible goal line.

"Like us, he's frustrated that the cops' hands are tied." She declined to tell her parents Gage's choice words about how he'd handle Derek or Viper if he had five minutes alone with them. His vehemence worried Zoey. What *would* happen if Gage ever confronted her ex or the loan shark in person? She thought of Derek's battered face and shuddered.

"So what are you going to do?" her mother asked.

"You can't give either of them another penny, that's for sure!" Her father poked the arm of the stuffed chair for emphasis.

"No, I won't. I promise." She turned to her

mother sorrowfully. "And I'll repay the money you loaned me. I swear."

"How?" her father asked.

Squaring her shoulders, she faced him again and stepped away from the window. "I was hoping the job at Bancroft Industries you offered me a couple years ago, before I left with Derek, was still available." She'd been reluctant to turn to her father for a job, loath to depend on him for help—again. But no other jobs had panned out, and she needed an income. When he hesitated, she rushed to add, "I know it will be entry-level because I haven't been to college, but...I plan to change that, too. After the baby comes, I want to get a degree."

He quirked a silver eyebrow. "In?"

Zoey wet her lips. "Well, theater has always been my first love. I know you don't think I can make a living as an actress, but—"

"Does it matter what I think?" her father asked, tilting his head.

Stunned by the question, Zoey opened her mouth. Closed it.

"I mean, sure," Neil continued, "I'm skeptical

about the kind of living you can make in the theater. But what do I know? I'm a stuffy old businessman. I know spreadsheets and profit margins, not scripts and curtain calls."

"Maybe you could teach acting, or help run a community theater?" her mother suggested.

She blinked at her parents, the first spark of excitement she'd known in month flickering to life inside her. "You'd be okay with that?"

"The real question is, would *you* be okay with it? You've been searching for yourself so long, sweetheart. We want you to find what you've been looking for. We just want you to be happy."

Happy? Zoey's heart tripped, and she cut a quick glance out the window to Gage. Somehow she couldn't picture any career, any education, any future making her happy if Gage wasn't there to share it.

What about what I need, Zoey?

"Of course there will always be a job of some sort for you with Bancroft Industries, if that's what you choose." Her father reached for her hand. "What's the point of owning a company if you can't practice a little nepotism?"

She gave him a sad grin. "You're not afraid I'll mess something up and embarrass you with the company?"

He shrugged. "Everybody screws up some-time."

She sighed. "Not you. Not Holly or Paige or Mom...*I'm* the black sheep of the family, the screwup."

"What?" Ellen said at the same time her husband scoffed, "Are you kidding me?"

Zoey cocked her head and pursed her mouth. "Shall we review my history?"

"Granted, you've made mistakes," Neil conceded, raising a hand. "But the rest of us have made our share, too. What matters is how you handle your screwup, how you fix it, how you own up to your mistakes."

Gage had said as much last night, too. Zoey bit down on her bottom lip. How was she supposed to fix all her mistakes with Gage?

Her father folded his arms over his chest. "Shall we review *my* shortcomings? I'd say the first one would be that I let you grow up feeling like you were a black sheep, instead of cherished for the unique, vibrant person you are."

"But Holly and Paige—"

"Are Holly and Paige. Don't compare yourself to your sisters. The three of you couldn't be more different from each other," her mother said. "Except in how much we love each of you."

Her father scratched his chin and tipped her a sheepish look. "You know, I've often wished I had more of your spontaneity and courage to take risks."

Zoey goggled at him. "What?"

He nodded. "I'm Mr. Conservative, Mr. Play-It-Safe. You know that. But many times I've had opportunities pass me by, both personally and in business, because I wasn't prepared to take the risk involved. Opportunities I now regret missing. Good or bad, you dive right in. You seize life with both hands and take a big bite."

"That's not always a good thing, Dad."

"I know. That's why you're in this pickle. But don't be so hard on yourself. Life is about finding a balance, honey. You just need to figure out how to make the most of your strengths without turning them into vices. Be yourself, the Zoey we know and love, but—" he winked at her "—tone it down."

Her mother touched her arm. "And don't be afraid to ask for advice before you jump into something next time."

Zoey felt hot tears sting her eyes. She'd felt so alone, so lost to her family because of her mistakes for the past several years. Hearing that her parents forgave her, accepted her—flaws and all—was a much-needed balm to her heart.

She turned back to the window before her mother and father could see the moisture pooling in her eyes. Gage was sprawled on the lawn, breathing hard, while Miles and Pet chased each other around the yard. He was a good uncle. Would be a good a father some day. A good husband…

But had she expected any less? He'd already proven the very best of friends. A man of strength and character and loyalty.

She could only pray it wasn't too late to earn his forgiveness and do the right thing by him.

On the Saturday morning before Christmas, while Gage was in his woodworking shop in the garage sanding the dollhouse and Pet was watching TV, Zoey took advantage of the lull in activity to inventory the baby's layette. With her mother's generosity, Paige's planning skills and Holly's practical advice on infant needs, the baby's room was already well supplied.

Zoey refolded the stack of soft pastel sleepers and returned them to a drawer of the dresser Gage had recently refinished. She ran a hand over the smooth finish and sighed. Gage was putting so much love and effort into preparing furniture for the baby that he spent more time in the garage than he did in the house with her. And maybe that was the point. Avoiding her.

How had a friendship that had once been so easy, so comfortable become so strained and awkward?

Despite the many hours of woodworking and preparing a nursery for after the birth, Gage still talked as though Zoey would be leaving within weeks after the baby came. That had been the agreement from the beginning, and he was holding her to their bargain. She had no room to complain or second-guess, but...thoughts of leaving *hurt*.

The idea of not being around to wake Pet in the morning with hugs and kisses and distract her with silly stories while untangling the girl's unruly hair filled Zoey with a hollow ache. Her chest tightened knowing there was no point in painting the forest mural she wanted for her baby at Gage's house. Because this room she was filling with Winnie the Pooh mobiles and soft receiving blankets would not be her child's permanent nursery, the effort would be wasted.

But the deepest pain came from wondering what would happen to her tattered friendship with Gage after she left. If things between them were as tense as they were now, how much more distant would Gage become when they didn't have the forced proximity of sharing the same roof keeping them together?

The peal of the doorbell brought her out of her morose reverie.

"I'll get it!" Pet hollered from the front of the house.

"I'm coming, Squirt. Let me answer it." Quickly, Zoey stashed the last of baby clothes she'd been organizing and hurried down the hall.

She took a cleansing breath, determined to buoy her spirits. She still had about four months to patch things up with Gage before he kicked her and her baby to the curb. She might be able to change his attitude before—

Her mind blanked, rebelling at the sight that greeted her in the living room.

Viper.

And Derek.

Zoey gasped, her heartbeat slamming into overdrive.

"There she is," Pet chirped helpfully, waving a hand toward Zoey.

"Hey, Red." Viper stretched his mouth into an oily smile. "Miss me?"

Zoey sent a questioning glance toward Derek,

who returned a wan, apologetic grimace. "Sorry, he gave me no choice."

She forced her brain to work, despite the numbing dread that weighted her down like sand. Her first goal had to be getting Pet out of harm's way, keeping the child she loved like her own daughter safe. "S-Squirt, you need t-to leave."

"Why?" Pet whined, oblivious to the threat these men posed.

"Just go!" Zoey barked, letting her fear sharpen her tone. Her mind scrambled. *Gage.* Gage was in the garage. Would he hear her scream for help over the drone of his electric sander?

Zoey took a quick step toward Pet and grabbed her arm. Tugging the little girl away from Viper, she rasped, "Go now. Get Gage."

As soon as she gave Pet the directive, her mind balked. Did she want to bring Gage into the line of fire? She remembered how Gage had quivered with rage and barely suppressed violence the night she'd confessed her transgressions. *I can handle him.*

The thought of Gage going head-to-head with Viper chilled her to the marrow.

Pet turned to do Zoey's bidding, but Viper's hand snaked out and clamped down on Pet's thin arm. Alarm flared in the girl's eyes, and she struggled against his grip.

"Ow! Let go!"

Protective fury exploded in Zoey. She lunged toward Viper, planting a hand in his chest and shoving with all her strength. "Stay away from her!"

Viper staggered back a step but quickly righted himself. He glared daggers at Zoey, his eyes bloodshot and wild. Her pulse tripped. He looked...*high*. He sent a look to Derek and jerked his head.

Immediately, Derek stepped forward, seizing Zoey by the arms to drag her back from Viper.

"Stop it!" she hissed, wiggling and twisting to try to free herself. "Let go of me!"

"Please, Zoey, just do what he says." The desperate quality of Derek's tone inched her stress level up a notch.

"Zoey!" Pet wailed, reaching for Zoey with her free arm.

"Shut up, kid." Viper yanked hard, reeling Pet into a restraining hold around her waist.

Panic swelling in her chest, Zoey stretched a hand toward Gage's niece, desperate to save her. "No! Don't hurt her!"

"Come on, man, let the kid go. She's got nothing to do with this," Derek said.

"What happens to her is up to you." Viper narrowed a menacing look on Zoey. He seemed twitchy, on edge. "You do what I tell you, the kid goes free. If not..." he slid an arm around Pet's throat, like a python wrapping around its prey "...I'll snap her neck."

A fresh surge of fear and mama-bear protectiveness spurred Zoey to lurch toward Viper. Her attempt to reach Pet was thwarted by Derek's grip on her shoulders. When she continued struggling, Derek encircled her body, pinning her arms at her sides with his own. The scent of him filled her nose and turned her stomach. Memories of being held by this man while in the throes of sex flashed like lightning in her mind. The embrace that had once fueled a sense of intimacy now filled her with anxiety and loathing.

She shuddered. How could she have ever believed she loved Derek? How could his touch, which now made her skin crawl, have ever made her burn with desire the way a simple look from Gage could now?

She wanted Gage, desired him.

Her mind stumbled over that thought, but she couldn't dwell on it now, not with a more immediate threat at hand.

"You won't get away with this," she growled, curling her lip at Viper. "I told the cops everything."

Viper smirked. "I heard. I bet you thought it worked, too, that you'd seen the last of me 'cause I disappeared for a couple weeks, huh?"

Zoey tensed but kept silent. In truth, she'd been cautiously optimistic the past two weeks when Viper had been conspicuously absent.

He shrugged. "Matter of fact, I did spend a little time in lockup. Cops found a couple joints when I got pulled over for a DUI." He cocked his pierced eyebrow. "But I bonded out last night, and I need some cash. I knew you were the girl with the connections to hook me up."

Zoey's heart sank. *Not again.*

Gage was right. She'd fed a monster when she paid off Derek, and she would never be rid of him or Viper until she took drastic action.

"I figure ten grand will get me started." Viper's smug grin gloated his knowledge of her fear, his understanding that she'd do whatever she must to protect Pet and spare her family a scandal.

He'd simply miscalculated her determination to ensure these things happened on her own terms from now on.

Within Derek's restrictive hold, Zoey stiffened her spine and clenched her back teeth. "Not a chance. You won't get a penny from me. Ever."

Derek leaned close to her ear and pleaded, "Please, Zoey, don't mess around. Give him what he wants. Trust me, you don't want to make him mad."

A ball of cold fear settled in her gut, but she

firmed her resolve. She had to end this thug's reign of terror. "No."

Viper scowled, then with a sadistic sneer, he wound Pet's long hair around his hand and pulled her head back. "Oh, really?"

Tears filled Pet's dark eyes, and she screeched in pain. "Stop it! That hurts!"

Oxygen whooshed from Zoey's lungs. She had to make a stand, but not while Pet was still at risk. As much as she wanted to keep Gage safe, to avoid bringing him into this confrontation, which would certainly make the situation more explosive, Pet's safety was paramount.

She met the child's frightened gaze. "Louder, Pet! Scream!"

The girl needn't be told twice. When Pet loosed an ear-piercing shriek, Zoey added her voice. And prayed they were loud enough for Gage to hear.

Gage guided the sander down the gentle curve of the cradle's headboard, then stopped long enough to blow the sawdust away with a deep breath. He studied his handiwork for a moment, deciding whether the edges needed another pass.

The cradle, a surprise Christmas gift for Zoey, was really taking shape, but the pride and accomplishment he felt each time he finished a project was bittersweet this time. As well as the piece was turning out, as satisfied as he was with the intricate decorative detail he'd added, he knew that the cradle would likely not be used under his roof. Once the baby safely arrived, he fully expected Zoey to bolt and file for divorce.

It was probably for the best. The new awkwardness between them and deep hurt he read in her eyes when she looked at him, *if* she looked at him, spoke clearly for the damage done to the close relationship they'd once had. Staying together might kill their friendship completely. That truth was clear enough in recent weeks with her reticence, her distance. And he, in turn, had given her space to figure out what she wanted, where she would go from here.

He'd resigned himself to letting her go, quietly, no fuss, no muss. But his heart broke a little more every day as Zoey's due date, the end of their marriage drew closer. He'd give his name to Zoey's baby as he'd promised, but he wouldn't be around every day to see the child he already loved grow up.

Thank God for Pet and the opportunity he had to be such an integral part of his niece's life. Without her, he might be tempted to withdraw into a cave and lick his wounds.

He knew he should be preparing Pet for Zoey's departure, but he hated to spoil the time Zoey and Pet had left together. He could see the love and trust that had grown between the two wild women in his life. He smiled thinking of the maternal glow and affection reflected in Zoey's jade eyes when she read books to Pet at night, embellishing the stories with her own unique dramatic flair.

For all her restlessness and disdain for the mundane, Zoey had settled into their domestic routine in recent weeks and had even seemed… *happy* being Pet's surrogate mother. If only he could have made her truly happy as his wife, his lover, his soul mate.

He stared down at the humming sander in his hand and sighed. How long had he been standing here daydreaming and wasting electricity while the sander ran idly?

He thumbed the power switch, and the electric sander died with a fading whine.

But a high-pitched screech continued after the tool was off.

A scream.

Pet. And Zoey, too, from the sound of it.

A chill chased down his spine. Their combined voices, raised in a shriek that would wake the dead, was downright bloodcurdling.

He set the sander aside, shucked off his gloves and contemplated going inside to see what the ruckus was about.

But he stopped himself. No doubt the two drama queens were just playing some kind of high-volume game of make-believe. Just last week, Zoey had been a zombie chasing Pet so she could eat her brains. He'd worried the game would give Pet nightmares, but his niece had loved the creepy scenario and never lost a wink of sleep.

Shrugging and grinning at the pair's antics, he went back to work. One thing was for sure, after Zoey left, the house would be a lot quieter.

Flipping the cradle on its end, Gage smoothed a hand down one of the rockers and decided the edges needed more buffing. Jamming his hands back into his gloves, he flipped the power switch on the sander and got busy.

"Shut up!" Viper roared. Reaching behind him, he pulled a large black gun from under his shirt.

Terror froze Zoey's vocal cords. She didn't know enough about guns to identify the make or model of the weapon in Viper's hand, but she knew its capacity. She knew how volatile Viper might be if he was high—how lethal.

When Pet continued screaming, he aimed the gun at Zoey. "Tell her to shut up!"

"P-Pet, stop!" Zoey choked out.

Pet angled her head and gasped when she saw the weapon. Her screams subsided to a whimper of fear.

"Don't try that again, bitch. I'm runnin' out of patience with you."

Terrified what Viper might do next, Zoey dug her fingernails into the arm Derek still had wrapped around her chest. With a hiss, he jerked free of her grip and moved his locked arm across her round belly.

"Please, just let her go and then...w-we can talk." Zoey's knees shook, and her mind spun. How was she supposed to get them out of this without giving Viper any more money?

Viper released the fist of Pet's hair he'd pulled taut, but rather than let her go, he scooped her up, under his free arm. "So you're ready to deal?"

Zoey tried to force air into her leaden lungs. She couldn't give this leech what he wanted. She'd promised Gage, promised her parents. Promised herself not to make any more stupid mistakes. He'd only keep coming back until he'd bled her dry. But how could she refuse him while he had Pet in a death grip?

Where was Gage? *Please, God, I need help!*

Maybe if she stalled, bought some time...

"I'll d-do what I can to get you some—"

"Sonofa—!" Derek snatched his arm from her waist and stumbled from behind her with a stunned look on his face. "What...what was that?"

Already rattled as she was, the odd look on Derek's face unnerved her. "What was what?"

He stared at her belly, as if only then realizing she was with child. "I felt something. It was freaky, like...something was moving..."

She blinked, needing a second to figure out what had spooked Derek. And then her baby kicked again, stretching and moving in her womb.

"Man, stop screwin' around," Viper snarled. He shifted his weight impatiently. "We don't have time for this."

Zoey stared at Derek's pale face, could practically see the gears clicking and connecting the dots in his head.

She held her breath and murmured, "That was the baby. He kicked."

Derek's gaze snapped up to hers, and for the first time in more than a year, she glimpsed the man she'd fallen for. The man she'd believed in enough to follow around the country while he chased rainbows and gambled away her inheritance.

"Red, do we have a deal?" Viper snapped. "Ten grand? I want it today. Cash."

Zoey divided her attention between Viper and Derek, the confusion in his eyes.

"The baby…" He wet his lips, and his Adam's apple bobbed as he swallowed. "My baby…"

Still holding Derek's gaze, she nodded and twitched a strained smile. Reaching for his hand, she laid his palm on her belly. "You felt him kick. He's waking up from a nap. Probably all the screaming woke him."

Derek's expression was nothing short of awe-struck. "It's a boy?"

"Not officially. But I have a hunch."

The baby wiggled inside her again, and Derek's eyes widened. "Whoa."

"Hey!" Viper barked. "Save the touching reunion for Oprah, people. I want my money, damn it!"

Zoey cast a nervous side glance toward Viper.

The muscles in his jaw jumped as he clenched his teeth, and his fingers tightened around the butt of the gun.

Silent tears tracked down Pet's cheeks as she dangled from Viper's restrictive underarm hold.

"Zoey," Derek started, his voice soft. "I didn't—"

"Hey!" Viper shouted, louder this time. Agitated. "I said cut the crap! I want my money!" Swinging the gun to the side, he fired a shot into the sofa next to where Zoey stood.

Pet gave a staccato scream.

Zoey yelped. Stumbled back. Fell against Derek.

Viper lifted the gun and resighted it.

Toward Zoey's heart.

Gage jerked his head up and quickly silenced the sander.

He could have sworn that loud pop sounded like a gun being fired. He set the power tool aside, listening carefully. But heard nothing else.

Twisting his mouth in indecision, he debated

whether he should check on Zoey and Pet. Whether he should call the police. Firing a gun in a residential area was illegal, after all. But was the noise a gunshot? Or had a transformer blown? A firecracker exploded?

Coupled with the screaming he heard earlier from Zoey and Pet, the loud noise had him on edge.

Then another loud shout reached his ears from inside his house. A male voice. Hostile. Angry.

Gage ripped off his gloves and rushed toward the back door.

"Hey, take it easy, man!" Derek said raising his hand toward Viper in a conciliatory gesture. "You don't need the gun. Zoey's gonna cooperate." He jerked a glance toward her. "Aren't you?"

Zoey's heart raced a million miles an hour, and her head buzzed in fear and confusion. Even if she wanted to cooperate, where was she supposed to get ten grand by tonight? She refused to take any more money from Gage or her parents. Viper wouldn't stop demanding money until they were all in the poorhouse.

Viper shot her a glare that demanded an answer.

How could she deny the thug his demands while he held Pet with one hand and a gun in the other?

"I—I don't have—"

Viper bit out a curse and huffed his irritation. "I'm sick of your stalling. Maybe a bullet in your gut would convince you I mean business."

He thumbed back the hammer, and the click of the cocking weapon rang like a death knell in Zoey's ears.

"No!" she rasped, staggering back into Derek's chest.

In surreal slow motion, Zoey watched Viper narrow his gaze with dark intent, tighten his grip on the gun, flex his finger around the trigger. Derek shoved her aside. She saw the flash of the muzzle. Heard the deafening blast.

She tumbled to the floor, crashing with a bone-jarring jolt.

Derek crumpled on top of her.

Stunned, the air knocked from her lungs by the fall, she stared up at Derek's face, his expression contorted. With pain, she realized a beat later.

Pet's wail of fear filled her ears. Echoes of the gunshot faded. She stared numbly at Derek, her brain slowly registering the unreal images swimming before her.

"Zoey," Derek rasped, "tell my...kid...I..." His eyes fixed, and light faded from his gaze.

Her heart stilled. Derek...

"Shut up, you brat!" Viper raged.

She heard Pet's yelp of pain, and with a reviving gasp of air, Zoey rallied, a shot of adrenaline clearing the fog of shock.

She rolled out from under Derek. Saw the blood spreading on his chest. Tasted bile surge into her throat.

Her mind spun, processing...

Derek had been shot. He was dead. He'd... saved her. Saved their child.

Noise.

Gage's voice. Calling to her. Pet screaming.

"I said shut the hell up!"

The angry shout reverberated like a crack of lightning through her brain.

Zoey spun toward Pet, lunging at Viper.

He re-aimed his weapon. The gun fired again. A train rammed into her ribs, knocking her backward.

Then pain.

Gage assessed the scene in a shattered second.

Derek was shot, probably dead.

Pet in the hoodlum's grip.

Zoey lunging at the tattooed man with the weapon…

Acting purely on instinct, the need to protect his family, he took two running steps toward Zoey before—

The blast of the gun stopped him in his tracks. Icy fear raced through Gage.

His wife slumped to the floor.

"Zoey!" Terror, spiked with rage, ripped through him. He charged.

Swinging around to meet his attack, the

gunman released Pet, squared his feet and aimed the gun with both hands.

At a fire scene, Gage shut off the part of his brain that naturally recoiled from the lethal capacity of flames and toxic smoke. He switched into a mode that operated purely on training and a sense of duty. Regardless of personal risk, he did his job.

Now, as he rushed the bastard in his living room, racing headlong at the muzzle of the thug's gun, Gage gave no thought to danger. His actions were fueled by an explosion of emotions long buried. Hatred for his abusive father. Fear of losing his family. Love for the woman who'd held his vulnerable heart since eighth grade.

He only knew he would die before he let this ass with the gun take what was his.

With a primal roar, Gage barreled forward, hands outstretched. Tackling the thug with the force of a linebacker, he grabbed for the gun and shoved the muzzle up. They crashed into the Christmas tree Zoey had set up last week. Glass balls and candy canes rained onto the floor, shattering.

"Gage!" Zoey cried over Pet's terrified sobs.

He didn't spare them a glance. His focus remained locked on the weapon clenched in Viper's hand. Gage had the thug's wrist in a vise grip, pinned to the wall, keeping the weapon raised, angled away from them. With his other arm, Gage tried to subdue Viper's free hand, which clawed and shoved at him.

He heard the shuffle of feet as Zoey sent Pet out the front door to the neighbors' house. "Tell them to call 911!"

The quiet gasps and sobs that filtered to him between Viper's snarls and his own grunts told him Zoey hadn't taken the same opportunity to escape.

Gage didn't know martial arts moves like the characters in movies used. His parents couldn't afford the *en vogue* lessons his classmates had all taken growing up. But his training with the fire department kept him in top physical form, and surviving his father had given him a black belt in down-and-dirty street fighting.

When Viper twisted, Gage turned. When

Viper punched, Gage dodged. When Viper grabbed, Gage elbowed.

An uppercut. A close-quarter jab. A twisted arm. Gage gave as good as he got, all the while struggling, until his arm shook with exertion, to keep Viper's gun out of the equation.

But Viper's arm was weakening, too. Hoping to make him drop the weapon, Gage smashed the loan shark's hand against the wall. Again. Again.

Viper grunted, growled. The gun fired, and plaster from the ceiling littered the floor.

Just when Gage thought he might be getting the upper hand, Viper head-butted his face. Gage's nose shattered. Pain exploded in his sinuses. Black spots danced in his vision.

And his grip on the thug's gun hand faltered. As Gage tried to blink away the stars blinding him, Viper wrenched his arm free. Cracked the butt of the weapon against Gage's skull. Fresh paroxysms of pain splintered his head.

His knees buckled, but Gage stayed on his feet. Barely.

Had to. Keep. Fighting.

Protect Zee.

His head pounded. Spun dizzily.

"Gage!" Zoey sobbed.

The steely muzzle of the gun jabbed Gage's ribs.

He gritted his teeth. And braced for the bullet.

Pain radiated through Zoey's torso, and warm, sticky blood seeped through the fingers she clutched over the bullet wound. Slumped on the floor, she rebelled at the notion that she'd been shot. That she was dying. How could this be happening?

With a sick heart, she watched Gage grapple with Viper, hating that he'd been drawn into the web of danger.

Help him.

She tried to push to her feet but couldn't. She was bleeding hard, getting so weak.

Gage.

At least, she'd had the presence of mind to get Pet out of the house. She could die knowing the girl she loved like her own was safe. But…

If she died, so would her baby.

A sob rose in her throat. Of all of her failures, letting her baby die would be the worst. She couldn't allow that to happen. Wouldn't. With shaking hands, she fumbled for something, anything to staunch the bleeding.

Derek's foot was near her head. Derek. Who'd died saving her and their baby from Viper's bullet.

She pulled his shoe off his foot and tugged on his sock.

Weak. So weak.

She ignored the fiery pain that ricocheted through her when she yanked harder on the sock. Finally it slid free off his heel, and she waded it into a ball. Jammed the material against her throbbing wound.

A gunshot blasted through the room. Terror-born adrenaline surged through her veins. Her gaze darted to Gage.

Please, God, no!

Both men were still on their feet, still battling.

Viper smacked his head into Gage's face,

and blood squirted from Gage's nose. Rage exploded in her. She flashed to high school, all the times Gage had shown up at her house with black eyes, a cut chin, a bloodied lip courtesy of his father.

She'd been helpless to do anything but offer a shoulder to cry on, an ice pack and butterfly bandage to repair the damage.

But she'd be damned if she'd let Viper pummel Gage without doing everything in her power to help the man she loved.

The man she loved.

Zoey sucked in a sharp breath and struggled to her feet, her muscles fueled by adrenaline and stubborn Bancroft determination. Pain and exertion beaded a sheen of sweat on her skin. Her legs shook. Her heart thundered in her ears.

She blinked hard, fighting back the black spots that crowded her vision. She had to stay conscious. For her baby.

For Gage.

Bracing an arm against the back of the sofa, she gave the scene a quick scan. What could she do? How could she help?

Viper had gained control of the gun. Zoey's blood froze as the thug jammed the weapon in Gage's ribs.

No!

Funneling every ounce of her remaining strength, Zoey grabbed a ceramic Santa from the end table. In one arcing motion, she hefted the decoration and cracked it against Viper's head.

The clatter of glass shattering and the thump of Viper's body hitting the ground were the last sounds she heard before darkness veiled her eyes.

Chapter 13

"Zee, can you hear me?"

Zoey climbed through the haze of pain, reaching for the voice that called to her. Gage's voice.

Blinking dry, scratchy eyes, she brought the faces that hovered over her into focus. In addition to Gage, two unfamiliar men watched her with concerned expressions. The room they were in rocked and bumped. A siren wailed.

She angled her gaze to take in the blinking monitors and bags of fluid hanging beside her. Even that much movement sent pain streaking through her.

An ambulance. They were in an ambulance. Because she'd been shot.

The entire terrifying incident replayed in her memory, bringing with it the same suffocating fear, the heart-rending grief and guilt. Her fault. It was her fault.

Warm fingers stroked her face. "Hey, that's it. Stay with me, baby."

Baby.

She gasped and dragged a hand to her belly. "The baby—" she rasped.

"Is okay," Gage answered, his voice breaking.

"We think the bullet missed your uterus," one of the EMTs said. "But you've lost a lot of blood. We gotta get you into surgery to stop the internal bleeding."

"We're almost to the hospital, Zee. Hang in there."

She rolled her head to the side, bringing Gage into focus, pressing her cheek more snugly into the hand he cupped against her. Blood still leaked from his nose, smeared over his face where he'd obviously swiped at the flow. Bruises were darkening in the red imprints of

Viper's fist on his jaw and over his left eye. A narrow gash opened at his hairline. Her heart twisted seeing the evidence of the battering he'd taken. Because of her. The danger she brought down on them all.

She lifted a hand toward his face. "Your nose—"

"Forget me."

"He won't let us work on him until he knows you're okay," the other EMT said with a frown.

She pulled her brow into a scowl. "Gage—"

He wiped his nose with the back of his hand. "I'll be okay." Flashing her a wry grin, he added, "I've had worse, remember?"

An ache slashed through her chest, unrelated to Viper's bullet. "I remember."

He'd suffered so much. Because of his abusive father. Because of his distant mother.

Because of his selfish best friend.

The man she loved.

The ambulance lurched as it took a turn into the hospital drive. The bounce of the tires over the curb blasted another bolt of pain to her core. She hissed and squeezed her eyes shut.

"Can't you give her something for the pain?" Gage asked.

"They will once she's inside."

"No...the baby," she groaned.

The EMT patted her hand. "They're aware of your pregnancy, ma'am. Anything they give you will be safe for the baby."

Biting her lip, Zoey thought of all the pain she'd caused Gage over the years—leaving him after graduation night, the long periods of no communication while she traveled the country with Derek, pushing him away on Thanksgiving...

What about what I need, Zoey?

Her heart gave an anguished throb, and with a suffocating certainty, she saw what she had to do. For Gage. So that she couldn't hurt him any further.

She gritted her teeth and battled the sting of tears as her stretcher was unloaded from the back of the ambulance. Gage clung to her hand as she was rolled into the E.R.

New faces crowded around her as the E.R.

staff took over. And still Gage squeezed her hand.

"Zoey!"

She angled her head toward the familiar voice.

Holly appeared at her side, her face pale with worry and her eyes wild with fear. "Oh, my God! What happened?" Then without waiting for an explanation, "Mom and Dad are on the way. They called me when they heard you were being brought in."

Because Holly was already at the hospital keeping vigil over her son.

"Stand back, please," a nurse said, nudging Holly and Gage out of the way. She lifted Zoey's arm, injected something into the port of the IV on the back of her hand. Immediately a warm comfort flowed through her, easing her pain and making her eyelids droop.

Not yet!

"Gage—" she choked out.

He leaned close, ignoring the nurse's frown. "I'm here, Zee."

Her head felt thick, fuzzy. What had she needed to tell him?

"Not…a hippopotamus. I—I know…what you can give me…for Christmas."

A puzzled look crossed his face, even as moisture filled his bloodshot eyes. He blinked hard. Tugged a grin. "What's that, Zee? You name it."

The injected drug sucked her deeper into a light-headed haze. "A divorce."

An iron fist, cold and brutal, constricted Gage's chest. A bitter ache laid open his heart and sank to his core. He stumbled back numbly as the nurse shoved him aside to wheel Zoey off to surgery.

Holly placed a comforting hand on his arm, guiding him toward the waiting room chairs. "Oh, Gage, honey, she didn't mean it."

Dropping onto a formed plastic seat, he fought for a breath, battled the surge of disappointment and grief that had a stranglehold on his throat. Maybe if he refocused his thoughts on the police officers combing the crime scene that was his living room, the questions he still had to answer for the cops once his own injuries had been treated, he could keep his mind off Zoey's request. *A divorce.*

Holly sat beside him, gathering his hand into hers. "It was the drugs talking. It had to be. She loves you. I know she does."

Stiffly, he shook his head. "No."

He'd known this was coming, had long ago accepted their marriage would end...someday. Or so he'd thought.

But Zoey's request had caught him off guard, hit him when his defenses were down, when he was terrified she might not pull through, when he was already barely clinging to his composure. That's all it was. He just needed a minute to regroup, to shove his raw emotions back down in the safe, hidden corner of his soul.

"I mean, she was babbling about a hippopotamus, for Pete's sake. She didn't know what she was saying," Holly continued.

"I want a hippopotamus for Christmas..." *Zee sang, laughing.*

He groaned and covered her mouth with his

hands. *"Would you please stop singing that stupid song!"*

Hunching forward, Gage braced his elbows on his knees and propped his forehead on his palms.

A divorce.

To his horror, a tear leaked from his eye and plopped on the leg of his jeans. Followed by a drip of blood from his nose.

Holly saw the red stain and gasped. "Come on, Gage. Let's get you fixed up."

He let her tug him to his feet and followed her listlessly to the admission desk, where they were handed a clipboard with forms to complete.

"I'll do the paperwork. You go on back," his sister-in-law said, waving him toward a waiting nurse. Holly took his wallet, with all his personal data and insurance information, and returned to the waiting room chairs.

Half an hour later, she joined him in the treatment room where a doctor was stitching the cut on his forehead. He gaze darted to Holly, and his pulse kicked anxiously. "Any word on Zoey?"

She shook her head. "But our parents arrived a few minutes ago. They're upstairs waiting for news outside the O.R. And there is a police officer waiting out in the hall to talk to you, to take your statement."

He sighed his frustration.

"Hold still, please," said the doctor stitching his head.

With a crease of worry in her brow, Holly stared at him, taking in the wads of cotton jammed in his nostrils to stop the bleeding and the splint taped to his broken nose. He'd been given a mild painkiller for his body aches, and a local anesthetic for his stitches. But his greatest pain couldn't be fixed with pills.

A divorce.

"All done." The doctor dropped his tweezers on a tray and snapped off his latex gloves. "I'll be back with your discharge papers in a second."

As the doctor disappeared into the hall, Holly took the stool he'd vacated and put a hand on Gage's knee. "Don't do this."

He angled a side glance at her. "Do what?"

"Divorce Zoey."

"It's what she wants." He lowered his gaze to the bloody gauze on the tray beside her.

"I don't think it is."

"Yeah, it is. Getting a divorce was always the plan. After her baby came." He shrugged, pretending the idea of letting Zoey go didn't fill him with a leaden grief. "We're just moving the date up."

Holly dragged both hands through her hair and growled. "Jeez! You two are the stubbornest, hardest-headed people I've ever—" Huffing out a deep breath, she grabbed his chin and made him give her his full attention. "I know you love her. That you've been in love with her since high school."

Gage jerked. "How—"

She scoffed. "Oh, come on, Gage. We're not all as blind as my sister. It's in your eyes every time you look at her. Besides, why else would you've put up with all her shenanigans for all these years?"

Gage held his breath. "What do you mean?"

"I mean loyalty is one thing. You've got that

in spades. I admire you for sticking by her, for helping her out of tight spots and giving her chance after chance when she takes you for granted. But you've been giving her her way for years, and it is time to say *enough*. Don't let her do this to you." Holly squeezed his knee, her expression and tone imploring him. "You don't want a divorce. I know you don't. I could see it in your face when she dropped her little Zoey bomb back there." She hitched her head toward the E.R. corridor. "Tell her it is time for your relationship to move forward on *your* terms."

He shook his head. "I can't *make* her love me."

"You don't have to. She already does."

"Not as a husband. Just as a *friend*." He spat the word out like a curse.

Holly puckered her forehead and sighed. "Are you sure? That might have been true in high school but…"

She glanced away, clearly planning a new attack, and Gage took his cue to leave. Sliding stiffly off the exam table and to his feet, he retrieved his jacket from a nearby chair.

"Look, Holly, I appreciate your concern, but my relationship with Zoey is…complicated."

She stood and faced him with a sorrowful face. "It doesn't have to be."

Shoving his arms into his coat, he grimaced. "I'm…not even sure we're still the friends we used to be."

Holly stepped closer and seized the sleeves of his jacket. "Gage, if you love her, fight for her."

"What do you think I've been doing since eighth grade?" He let frustration sharpen his tone, but Holly didn't back down.

"You've been waiting. Patiently waiting for Zoey to wake up to what you two really have together. But you've let her steer the ship, and you should know better than anyone that Zoey leads with her heart instead of her head. She's been drifting for years, trying to figure out what she wants, who she is. You've let her keep you on hold, waiting in the wings, even when she was off chasing rainbows and following false leads. For some reason I don't understand, she can't see what is painfully obvious to everyone around her. You're the world to her, Gage. She loves you."

He wanted to believe Holly was right. Wanted it more than his next breath. But how long could he go on hoping, waiting, praying for something that might never be? If Holly was wrong...

"Gage, just...promise me you won't do anything...yet. Once she's on the mend—" Her voice cracked, and she closed her eyes. "Dear God, let her mend—and we get this mess with Derek and the loan shark from Las Vegas straightened out—"

He snapped his gaze to hers. "You know about that?"

"Only recently." Her cheek lifted in a small grin. "There are no secrets with the Bancroft sisters. You know that." She took his hand. "When things settle down and she's out of the hospital, promise me you'll be up-front with her about how you feel, lay everything out in the open with her. *Everything.*"

His heart rose to his throat, but he squeezed her fingers back. "I promise."

* * *

"Well, I think that covers it." The Lagniappe P.D. homicide detective flipped his notebook closed and rose from the chair beside Zoey's bed. "Thank you for your time, ma'am."

"Detective Raneau?" Zoey said, bunching the hospital-bed blanket in her fingers. "What happened to Viper? Did he bond out? Could he come after us for revenge?"

Raneau pressed his mouth in a taut line. "No, ma'am. He's not going anywhere. The judge denied him bail. He'll be a guest of the parish until he's prosecuted for Derek Fremont's murder, and three accounts of attempted murder." He tipped his head to the side. "Along with various lesser charges. You don't need to worry about him hurting you or your family again."

"Thank goodness!" Zoey's mother said with a relieved sigh.

Zoey nodded her thanks to the detective as he stepped out into the hall.

Turning to her mother, who had been at her side ever since she'd left surgery several hours ago, Zoey pressed the button on the bed controls to crank her mattress to a sitting position. "I'm so glad that's over."

Her father scooted his chair closer to the bed, making room for the rest of the family as they poured through the door from the corridor. "We all are, honey. You gave us quite a scare."

Viper's bullet had left a gash in her left side below her ribs. A little deeper than most flesh wounds, the gash had required only stitches and a round of antibiotic for good measure. But her obstetrician had requested she be kept for observation. So far so good.

Zoey scanned the faces as they assembled around her bed—Paige and Jake, Holly and Matt…but no Gage. Her heart sank. She needed him, needed to reassure herself he was all right. She had the oddest unsettled sensation in the pit of her stomach that something was wrong. Something terrible was unresolved between them.

"Where's Gage?" she asked the crowd. She'd seen him briefly as they wheeled her up to her room. He'd stuck around the hospital only long enough to get a report on her condition, before heading back to retrieve Pet from the neighbor who was keeping her. And deal with the cops processing the scene of Derek's murder.

She shuddered. Derek was *dead.*

"Gage is at Mom and Dad's house with Pet," Holly said. "He thought she needed some special attention in light of what she'd seen today."

Zoey frowned, though she understood the little girl probably needed her uncle more than Zoey did. The early reports she'd gotten from the family and police said that Pet was shaken but coping as well as could be expected.

"Kids are resilient, Zoey," Matt said. "We'll all give Pet the love and security she needs in the coming months, and I have no doubt she'll be fine."

Her pediatrician brother-in-law's reassurance eased Zoey's mind, but she was anxious to hug Pet for herself and tell the little girl how proud she was of her bravery and assistance in calling for help.

"Well, we know it's been a pretty traumatic day, and you need to rest," Jake said and squeezed her toes through the bed covers. "We'll get out of your hair."

"Actually…" Paige said and exchanged a meaningful look with Holly. "I think Holly and I are going to stick around a few more minutes. We want to talk to Zoey about something… important." Jake gave his wife a puzzled look, but she dismissed him with a jerk of her head toward the door. "In private."

"I'll be with Adam when you finish here," Matt told Holly and gave her a kiss. Then to his mother-in-law, "That leaves a free seat in the PICU if you want to hold your grandson. The nurses say he gained another ounce since yesterday."

"He's up to four pounds, thirteen ounces now," Holly said, beaming. "Just three more ounces, and he can come home."

Her family cheered Adam's good news as they disbursed.

Zoey smiled. Adam's progress had been remarkable. An answered prayer. Surreptitiously, she slid a hand to her belly. Her own miracle. The doctor had assured her that with plenty of rest and attention to her own recovery, he saw no reason the pregnancy wouldn't proceed normally.

Derek had saved her. Saved her baby. And Gage had gotten her to the hospital when she was dying. She wished he were here now... Bittersweet gratitude brought a lump to Zoey's throat.

"You all right, darling?" When Ellen hesitated, Neil nudged her toward the door.

"Go on, Grandma. Let our girls have their powwow."

"I'll be back in a little while, sweetheart," her mother said, pressing a kiss to Zoey's forehead.

Holly and Paige took the chairs beside Zoey's bed as the rest of the family exited and scooted in close. Their expressions warned her she was in for a serious lecture.

Zoey's pulse picked up, and the monitor beside her bed beeped faster in turn. "What's going on?"

Paige scooped Zoey's hand into hers and pinned an all-business look on her sister. "Holly told me you asked Gage to give you a divorce for Christmas."

Zoey's stomach lurched. "I did *what?*"

Holly frowned. "You don't remember? Right before they took you into surgery?"

Zoey's breath stuck in her lungs. Images flashed through her memory.

Gage's bloody nose. "Can't you give her something for pain?"

An E.R. nurse. "Stand back, please."

"What's that, Zee? You name it."

"Oh, God..." she whispered, her heart giving a painful twist.

"Why would you do that?" Paige asked, her tone gently scolding. "Don't you know how much that man loves you?"

"I...I—" she stuttered, dividing a glance between Paige's baffled expression and Holly's worried frown. She fumbled to gather her composure, her thoughts, and to make sense of the jumbled emotions knotting her chest. "It's...not a real marriage. We had an agreement...from the start." She paused long enough to swallow, loosening the constriction in her throat.

"In fact, being married has…nearly ruined our friendship."

Squeezing her eyes closed, Zoey sucked in a deep breath, fighting the wave of pain her admission brought.

"How do you mean?" Paige shifted from the chair to sit on the edge of the bed.

"There's tension between us that was never there before. Not like this anyway."

"Isn't that understandable, considering all this mess you were in with that Viper guy stalking you and Derek demanding money?" Paige asked.

"Maybe. I know most of the blame is mine."

"I didn't say that!" Paige countered, squeezing her hand tighter. "Don't waste time pointing fingers or feeling guilty. That trouble is behind you. Your job now is to save your marriage."

Zoey lowered her gaze to pluck at a loose thread in the hospital blanket. "How? We hardly even talk anymore."

"Well, there's your first step to fixing this," Holly said. "You need to tell Gage what you're feeling."

Zoey sank deeper into her pillows and drew her eyebrows together. "I wish I knew what I felt. I've got so many things jumbled up inside me. Weird feelings that confuse me and scare me. Conflicting feelings that I can't begin to understand…"

Paige sat straighter. "Then let's analyze them, figure things out."

Zoey twitched a grin at her sister. Analysis was Paige's answer to everything.

"Do you love Gage?" Holly asked, leaning closer, cutting to the heart of the matter.

"Of course I do. He's my best friend!" Zoey hesitated, a pluck of despair pinching her. "At least he used to be. I'm not sure what we are now."

Holly tipped her head. "It's understandable for a relationship to change when you go from a platonic relationship to being lovers. Sex changes things."

Zoey snapped a startled look to her sister, her pulse pounding. "What?"

Paige narrowed a speculative look on Zoey.

"You two have become lovers since marrying, haven't you?"

Memories of Thanksgiving night crowded Zoey's brain. "I—not exactly. I...made it a term of our arrangement. No sex."

Holly and Paige exchanged looks of dismay.

"Why not? Aren't you attracted to him?" Holly asked.

"My gosh, Zoey! The man is *hot*. What's not to like?" Paige added.

Remembering how sexy Gage looked in nothing but his sleep pants Thanksgiving night, Zoey felt her mouth go dry. "That's not the point."

Paige folded her arms over her chest. "Then clue us in. I, for one, am lost."

Zoey twisted the string on her blanket so hard that the thread snapped off in her hand. She gnawed her bottom lip and gave her sisters a sheepish glance. "Remember how I left for Europe the day after I graduated high school?"

"Yeah," Holly replied. "It was kind of abrupt, but we figured it was typical Zoey spontaneity. Why?"

"Gage and I…slept together on graduation night."

Holly's eyebrows shot up, and Paige's jaw dropped.

"And?" Holly prodded.

"That's what my leaving for Europe was about. I ran from him."

Paige winced. "The sex was that bad?"

Tears filled Zoey's eyes. "No. It was that good."

Holly stroked the hair back from her sister's forehead. "Zoey, why did you run?"

"I was scared."

"Of what? Gage?" Paige scooted closer.

"Of what I felt for him that night. Scared of what it would mean for our friendship. When I made love to him, I felt things so deep and raw and pure that…I didn't know what to think. Was it just because I'd been a virgin? Was I imagining the feelings? Would he feel the same way? How would it change our friendship? What if he regretted it? What if it hadn't meant the same thing to him and he broke my heart? What if he thought it was a mistake and he couldn't face me again? What if—"

"Oh, Zoey," Paige said on a sad laugh. "And you two tease *me* for analyzing things to death!" She sobered then and laced her fingers with Zoey's. "The first time Jake and I made love, while we were on the run together last summer, I felt a lot of the same things you're describing. Like Hol said, sex changes things. I knew I loved Jake, but I had no idea what would happen to us, what he felt for me, if our lovemaking had been as significant to him as it was to me."

Zoey nodded. "The next morning, more than anything else, I was scared I'd say or do something to screw up our friendship. I didn't know how to face him. So...I ran." She huffed a sigh. "Maybe I'm still running. Cowardly, I know, but..."

"Zoey." Holly's tone was as serious as she'd ever heard it. "Whatever happened back then, whatever has happened since then, whatever is going on now between you and Gage, the thing that matters is how you *feel* about each other. I think you've *both* been running scared since that night, so scared of losing each other if you rock the boat that you tiptoe around the truth and shield your eyes from looking too closely at what you've got together."

The man I love.

Zoey swallowed hard. Took a breath. "I...I think I love him."

A bright smile lit Holly's face. "I know you do. Tell *him*."

When the baby showed no signs of distress after forty-eight hours, Zoey was allowed to go home. Other than general soreness at the wound site, mitigated by the prescription-strength acetaminophen her doctor ordered, and normal posttrauma fatigue, Zoey felt remarkably good. Even though Gage questioned her doctors about the quick discharge, Zoey was anxious to get home—"home" being her parents' house until Gage's living room was released as a crime scene and thoroughly cleaned. She was eager as well for some time alone with Gage, an opportunity to talk privately.

But as they had from the moment they

received word of her injury, Zoey's family gathered around her as she left the hospital. She struggled for patience, which had never been a virtue of hers, as Gage drove her, Pet and Zoey's mother to the Bancroft estate.

Zoey cast a glance across the front seat at her husband's bruised and bandaged face, and her chest tightened with remorse for his injuries. "After we drop Mom and Squirt off, can we go to our house and let me pack up a few things?"

"I already packed you a bag. It's at your parents'."

"Please?" She pushed the glasses she'd opted for over her contacts while in the hospital back up her nose. "I want…to pick some things for myself."

"Can it wait, honey? The doctors want you to rest, take it slow for a while," her mother said.

She met Gage's inquiring look with a steady, meaningful gaze. And no further explanation was needed. He nodded his understanding. They needed a chance to talk. Alone.

Ten minutes later, he pulled into his driveway and cut the engine. "Let's go in the back way.

The front room is still—" Rather than finish, he sighed, glanced down at his hands which clutched the steering wheel in a white-knuckled grip.

With a deep breath, Zoey gathered her courage, bracing herself to face the evidence of violence in the house. Preparing for the conversation she needed to have with Gage. Her request for a divorce still hung between them. She'd been waiting for a private moment with him to clear the air in that regard. But how would he react? Was it too late to save their friendship, much less their marriage?

He offered his arm to steady her as they entered the kitchen through the back door, then she released her grip on him to shuffle to the kitchen counter and discard her purse beside a stack of accumulated mail. An envelope bearing the return address of a local law firm sat on top of the pile.

Zoey's lungs seized as she picked it up and turned to him. "What's this?"

Gage stilled when he saw what was in her hand, and his expression darkened. "You weren't supposed to see that...yet. It was going to be your Christmas present."

I know what you can give me for Christmas...

Her heart sank, and the optimism she'd had since her talk with her sisters dimmed. She set the envelope back on the counter with a trembling hand and raised tear-puddled eyes to Gage. "That was quick."

He frowned. "Not really. I started the process two months ago. They were supposed to have the papers to us to sign weeks ago."

She bit her bottom lip to keep it from trembling. Took a moment to battle down her shock and disappointment. "You talked to a lawyer back in *October?*"

Even though a divorce had been the agreement from the start, it hurt to think he'd been so eager to start the process that many months before her baby was due.

Gage shrugged awkwardly, shifted his feet. "Well, yeah."

She braced a hand on the edge of the counter when her legs wobbled. Gage took a quick step toward her, and she held up a hand to keep him back. "I'm okay. I just—"

Tell him.

Drawing a deep reinforcing breath, she locked her knees and squared her shoulders. Grabbing up the envelope, she ripped it in half, then quarters and let the pieces flutter to the floor. "I don't want a divorce, Gage. I'm sorry. I know that's what we agreed on before we married, that it was one of the terms we laid out, but… things have changed," she blurted, shaking all over. "I know you're mad at me for not telling you everything about Viper and Derek and for giving them money without talking to you, and you have every right to be mad."

Gage squatted and picked up the pieces of the letter she'd torn up, while she continued without so much as a breath. "I know I'm hard to live with. That I'm shortsighted sometimes and too impulsive and emotional—although, to be fair, a lot of my weepiness lately has been because of stress and because I'm pregnant. But if you'll give me another chance, I'll try to do better. I'm trying to change. I mean, the fact that I'm telling you how I feel now and not avoiding the issue any longer is part of my attempt to change."

She was prattling. She knew it. But Gage was thumbing through the torn pieces of the document from the lawyer as if looking for something, and his silence was making her nervous.

"I talked to Holly and Paige the other night, and they helped me see what I'd been trying to deny for years. I was just so scared that if I admitted the truth, to myself or to you, that everything would fall apart, and I'd lose the best friend I'd ever had. I guess I ran from you because it was better somehow than having you run from me if you knew how I really felt."

Gage's hands stilled on the scraps of paper he'd been shuffling.

Zoey gulped a lungful of oxygen and gripped the edge of the countertop harder. "The thing is, Gage...I love you."

He jerked his head up, met her gaze, his expression stunned.

She swallowed hard, her heart thundering. "As in *love* love. And I want to be your wife."

He was silent for several taut seconds.

"So…" Her attempt at a smile fell short. "Say something."

He blinked and dropped his attention to the scraps of the document in his hand. "I wish you hadn't ripped this up without looking at it first. I hope we don't have to wait two more months to get another copy."

Pain slashed through her. "Gage—"

He held the scraps out to her. "Read."

When she hesitated, he held the pieces directly in front of her nose.

The words *petition for* and *biological mother* swam into focus. Confused, she grabbed the pieces from him and tried to line the text up in order.

"It's a petition to legally adopt your baby," he said, saving her the trouble of reconstructing the document. "All it needed was your signature and Derek's to make it final, to make your baby legally mine."

Now it was her turn to stare, shocked silent.

"If that's okay with you."

She nodded, tears stinging her eyes. "Yes. Please. I want you to be my baby's father."

"We can ask the lawyer for a new copy, of course, although…I'm not sure what the legalities are now that Derek—" He stopped. Jammed his hands into his back pockets and stepped back. "Well, Merry Christmas."

A deep breath shuddered out of her. "Leapin' lizards, Gage. I…thought they were divorce papers. I—"

"Yeah, about that…" He scratched his stubble-dusted chin. "That ain't happenin'."

Her pulse stumbled to a faster, hopeful cadence. "Really?"

"Really." His cheek dimpled, and humor lit his eyes. "I know it was what we agreed to in Vegas, but see…my plan all along was to change your mind about that. I've had my heart set on being your husband since eighth grade, so why, after eleven years of waiting for you, would I willingly let you go?"

Her brow puckered. "Eleven years?"

He closed the distance between them and slid an arm around her waist. "You heard me. I have loved you since drama class in eighth grade."

Zoey curled her fingers into the sleeves of his

shirt and shook her head, dumbfounded. "Why didn't you say anything?"

His eyes widened, and he made a choking sound. "Wha—I did! Plenty of times!"

Zoey scowled. "When?"

"Every time we hung up from a phone call."

She pulled a face. "That doesn't count. That's just part of our goodbye."

"It counted for me. And I said it graduation night, before we slept together."

She chuckled. "Because that's what guys say to girls to get in their pants."

He shook his head. "I meant it. And I said as much at our wedding."

She scrunched her nose. "When?"

"After the Elvis wannabe asked if I would love and cherish you till death do we part."

Zoey bit her bottom lip and thought back to that day, to the answer he'd given.

Absolutely, positively. Her heartbeat slowed.

"Leapin' lizards," she whispered, meeting his eyes as other comments he'd made through the years took on new meaning and understanding dawned.

He nodded. "Yeah." Then, "I love you, Zee. With all my heart."

She was crying again, though now with tears of joy. Joy so deep that she was shaking from the inside out, ready to burst with it.

"I've been so blind," she rasped, sliding off her glasses to swipe her eyes.

Gage took the glasses, dried the lenses on his shirt and slid them back onto her nose.

"I forgive you." He pressed a gentle kiss to her forehead. "But it's not all your fault. I didn't fight for you when you pulled away. I'm sorry. I guess I thought a guy like me—from the wrong side of the tracks, with a dysfunctional family tree—didn't deserve someone like you."

She tipped her chin up and quirked a grin. "You mean an impetuous drama queen with a tendency to screw things up?"

"I mean a vivacious, passionate beauty with a tendency to lead with her heart."

She wrapped her arms around his neck and brushed a soft kiss over his mouth. "Then I forgive you, too."

Gage stole another, deeper kiss, then murmured against her lips. "You know what I want for Christmas?"

She tipped an impish grin and threaded her fingers through the hair at his nape. "I have a pretty good idea, but...my doctor said I shouldn't for the next four to six weeks."

Gage snorted a laugh. "That's not what I meant. Although...the next six weeks are going to be torture."

She nipped his bottom lip, and he groaned.

"What, then? What do you want for Christmas? Name it."

Prying loose from her arms, he dropped to one knee and clasped one hand over his heart. "Marry me, Zoey Bancroft. Again. With all of our family there to share it and knowing that this time it is for real. For forever."

She gasped her delight. "That sounds perfect."

Epilogue

Six weeks later, on a mild February afternoon, Zoey knocked on her parents' pool-house door and waited impatiently. On the back lawn, white folding chairs were lined up and lacy ribbons and bows dressed the gazebo where she and Gage would renew their vows in—she checked her watch—less than an hour.

When he opened the door, Gage gave her a curious frown. "Isn't it bad luck for the groom to see the bride before the ceremony?" He sent a cursory glance over her bathrobe, and his frown deepened. "Shouldn't you be dressed by now?"

She pushed past him, grinning coyly, and checking the room to be certain he was alone. "One, we are already married, so I kinda think that superstition is moot. Two, I think you'll like what I have in mind."

He arched one dark eyebrow, and she sidled up to him, sliding her fingers along the satiny lapel of his tuxedo. "Do you know what today is?"

He closed the door and said wryly, "Uh…our renewal ceremony?"

She shrugged. "That, too." Reaching past him she flipped the lock on the door. "It has also been six weeks since I was released from the hospital."

Gage's eyes widened, and he tilted his head. "Zoey, what are you—"

Her seductive grin and nibbling kisses to his chin answered him. His Adam's apple bobbed, and she felt his muscles tighten under her hands.

"Sweetheart, we have one hundred guests arriving as we speak. The service—"

She stepped back from him, slid the bathrobe

off her shoulders and struck a come-hither pose...nude. "They can hardly start without us."

He stroked a hand over his mouth, his pupils dilating with desire. "Lordy, but you're beautiful."

"Even seven months pregnant?"

He smiled warmly. "Especially seven months pregnant."

Zoey pressed as close to his lean muscles as her pregnancy bump would allow and wrapped her arms around his neck. "Make love to me, Gage."

"They'll be looking for us." He stripped off his tuxedo coat and jerked loose the knot in his cravat.

She started on his shirt buttons. "The door is locked."

Gage toed off his shoes. "You're crazy, you know that?"

She giggled. "But you love me anyway."

"Damn straight. Don't ever change." His pants were discarded hastily, and his shirt followed the rest of his clothes to the floor. "You realize this is where we made love the first time, on graduation night?"

She threaded her fingers through his hair and flashed a seductive grin. "What better place to make love our second time, then?"

Brushing a kiss over his lips, she absorbed the shudder that raced through him. A crackling yearning pulsed through her, leaving her trembling and achy with need. She nipped at his earlobe and whispered huskily, "Please, I want to feel you inside me, Gage."

Muttering something terse under his breath, he scooped her into his arms and strode briskly across the room to the couch. He set her gently on the cushions, then straightened to skim his boxers to his feet. When they were both naked, they stared at each other for a few seconds, testing the moment six years in the making.

"You're sure?" he asked, like he had on graduation night.

She flashed a temptress smile and lowered her eyes to his impressive erection. "Oh, yeah."

Stretching out on the cool cushions, he curled his body around hers, careful not to crush her.

His hands explored her bare flesh, and his lips set fires wherever they touched her. He was tender and attentive, worshipping her with his fingers and his loving gaze.

For long minutes, she savored the feel of his warm skin and hard muscle grazing her body, and she returned his kisses with a fervor that spoke for the love swelling in her heart. But soon the thrum of desire pounding in her blood made her impatient with his caution.

Sinking her fingers into his lower back, she canted her hips forward and urged him home. "Now, Gage. I want—"

Her words caught in her throat as he buried himself inside her, growling his satisfaction. With his weight levered off her, he held her gaze and thrust again, harder, deeper. Filling her. Binding them. Blending their souls.

Whispering his name, Zoey shattered, flying apart in a starburst of the most exquisite sensation she'd ever experienced, taking Gage with her into the maelstrom of sweet release.

She'd wasted so much time searching for that certain something that would fill the longing inside her, tame her restless heart and bring her a lasting happiness and peace, only to discover she'd had what she was looking for all along. But now, still trembling in the wake of their passion, she knew she'd found the place where she belonged. Gage had always been her destiny, and she was finally home.

A knock at the door roused Gage from a sated lethargy, the blissful afterglow of mind-numbingly good sex. Great sex.

And he had his whole life ahead of him, with Zoey, to explore this explosive chemistry. Life was good.

"Gage?" Jake called from the other side of the pool-house door. "Dude, they're ready for us. You in there?"

He pressed a hand over Zoey's mouth to muffle her laugh. "Be right there!"

"Hey, Paige says she can't find Zoey. You have any idea where she is?"

Gage had to bite the inside of his cheek not to laugh and give them away. "Try the kitchen.

She's had a voracious appetite lately. She might be getting a snack."

Zoey laughed harder, and he had to kiss her to keep her from blowing their cover.

Jake didn't respond for a moment, then said, "Right. Eight minutes until showtime."

Seven minutes later, Gage took his place at the front of the rows of filled seats, aware that he had a sappy, satisfied grin on his face. Jake and Matt exchanged a knowing look, and Jake raise a hand to give Gage a fist bump. "You dog."

Matt leaned over and whispered, "Your tie is crooked, stud."

With a brief squeal of feedback through the amplifier, the uniquely Zoey-styled ceremony on the back lawn of the Bancroft family estate began. In lieu of a stately, traditional wedding march or subdued ballad, her sisters, carrying wild flowers, and Gage's sister Elaine—out of rehab and holding her own at one hundred twenty-seven days sober and counting—danced down the aisle to Sister Hazel's "All For You," which Zoey and Gage had loved since high school. Gage grinned at Elaine, pride for her dedication to a fresh start warming him from the inside out.

Neil Bancroft escorted his wife, who carried her first grandson, Adam—now six-plus pounds and thriving—to their seats in the front row.

Pet appeared at the microphone and, with the aplomb of a professional announcer, said, "Ladies and gentlemen, we have a special play we'd like to do for you. My aunt Zoey wrote it and helped us learn our parts."

Gage cast a curious glance toward his sisters-in-law, who looked equally bemused.

"Once upon a time," Pet said clearly, with a stage voice that boded a future in drama like her aunt, "there were three sisters. The oldest sister was smart and successful, but she picked the wrong man to marry and bad men stopped her wedding."

Pet put a white veil on her head, and Paige grinned.

"Luckily, a handsome prince was at her wedding to save her life," Pet continued.

Miles ran up to Pet and tried to pick her up. When that failed, he shrugged and grabbed her hand and dragged Pet across the makeshift stage.

The audience chuckled and applauded.

Next, Palmer appeared from "offstage," stepping out from behind a large bush beside the gazebo where the minister waited. "The middle sister married a nice man and moved far away." Miles played the groom again and marched with his sister to the other side of the stage.

"But the nice man died, and the middle sister was sad," Palmer said.

Miles sprawled on the floor, and Palmer burst into fake tears.

"Until a handsome stranger appeared, and she fell in love again!" Pet said.

"That's you, Dad!" Miles said grinning, as he jumped to his feet and hugged his sister.

"I got that," Matt returned, chuckling along with the rest of the crowd.

Gage watched the children scurry to their respective parents and smiled, anticipating the day he and Zoey would welcome their son—the ultrasound confirmed she was having a boy—

and future children together. He was part of a big, loving family and had never been happier.

"The youngest sister," Zoey said, making her entrance from offstage, "spent years traveling far and wide, looking for the kind of happiness her sisters had found."

Gage's heart leaped as his bride appeared, resplendent in a peach maternity cocktail dress with a filmy skirt and lacy bodice. She'd managed, in the few minutes since she'd sneaked out of the pool house and scurried back into the main house, to comb her hair and twist it into a loose knot with sprigs of baby's breath. She met his gaze and winked.

"The youngest sister made lots of mistakes and took lots of wrong turns as she searched for the man of her dreams." Zoey walked to center stage and smiled at Gage. "But through it all, she had a best friend who saw her through the ups and downs of her misadventures. She couldn't have asked for a more loyal or patient friend."

Pulse thumping, Gage stared, mesmerized,

as always, by the auburn-haired beauty who'd turned his life upside down in eighth grade.

"But the youngest sister was confused by her feelings for her friend, and to her everlasting shame, she hurt him many times before she woke up to the fact that the love of her life was right there all along. Not off in Europe or Las Vegas or any of the many points in between. The man who made her happier than she'd ever been, who made all her dreams come true and who made her burn with passion had been standing beside her from the very start."

Gage was fighting the lump growing in his throat, when she held her hand out and motioned for him to join her. He slipped his hand in hers and drew her close, as she continued, "When she finally wised up, she was afraid she was too late, terrified she lost her friend forever."

Gage shook his head and whispered for her ears only, "Never."

"But Fate intervened, and the youngest sister got another chance to show her friend that she'd finally found her way home." Tears sparkled in her green eyes as she tipped her face toward his.

"Gage Powell, thank you for all you've meant to me through the years and thank you for waiting for me to get my head on straight. I love you. Deeply. Honestly. Unconditionally. The way you've always loved me, even when I was too blind to see it. My heart belongs to you…for the rest of my life."

Gage held her gaze, held his breath.

A few seconds passed, then Zoey arched an eyebrow and leaned close, whispering, "This is the part where you kiss me and say you love me, too."

Love and happiness so powerful he couldn't contain them surged through Gage. He threw his head back, and a joyous laugh rolled up from his chest. Kissing his wife's smiling lips, he murmured, "I do love you, Zee. For always."

As their friends and family clapped and cooed, Pet jumped back onto the gazebo stage and shouted, "And they all lived happily ever after!"

* * * * *